THE GIRL WHO LOVED TOO MUCH

BY

MICHELLE GORDON

First published in Great Britain in 2020 by Jasper Tree Press
An Imprint of Not From This Planet

Cover Design by The Amethyst Angel & Magic Letterpress

ISBN: 978-1-912257-52-2

GRATITUDE

An ocean of gratitude to Jon, for the love, the support, the challenges and the giggles. I love you.

Love and gratitude to my mamma, Sally Byrne. She is everything to me, and I can only keep writing because of her unrelenting love and support.

So much gratitude for those who have loved and believed in me the longest; Liz Lockwood, Helen Gordon, Liz Gordon, Lucja Fratczak-Kay, Niki Gilbert, Roberta Smart, Kelly Draper, Sarah Rebecca Vine, Rachael Barnwell and Charlotte Tomkins. You are all angels (and Faeries!) to me. I love you.

Gratitude to Kenny John, of Creates Gallery, for being such a great friend and boss. Love you, SB!

So much love to Jess Bailey, for being such a fabulous housemate, and for inspiring me and cheering me on. Love you, Baby Bear!

Of course, this book would not have existed if it weren't for my new passion for letterpress printing. And for that, I have many people to thank. The printing community is without a doubt the most welcoming one I have ever encountered, and I have been met with nothing but encouragement and support. I'd love to thank Francesca Kay, and Sarah from Berrington Press for igniting the MAGIC spark, on that grey September day in 2019. Roger of Urban Fox Letterpress, Lisa of Lyme Bay Press and John of Pressing Matters Magazine, you have all enabled me to set up my studio and fill it with all sort of delights, which has brought me an endless amount of joy! Thank you also to everyone on Instagram in the print community, you guys are truly awesome.

Finally, huge virtual hugs to all my many readers, especially those who have become cherished friends, and those who have taken the time to write reviews, and send messages to let me know how much my books have helped them. Your love truly does keep me writing, so thank you, I love you. Here are just a few names, if I have missed you out, please write your name in the space below, because I love you too!

Tiffany Hathorn, Alex Lane, Shelley-Nicole Brookdale, Amanda Bigrell, Andrew Embling, George Hardwick, Xander Holland, Laurie Huston, Anabela Da Costa, Rosa Ivy, Chip Jenki[illegible]nette Ecuyere, Lesley George, Margaux Joy DeNador, Dudley DeNador, Philip James, Sharon Andrews, Jenni Riley, Vikki Elizabeth Finlay, Duane Brovan, Trish Mclean, Trisha & Bruce Barnes, Jacqueline Wigglesworth, Lou Brister, Nicky Lee, Annie Hartwright, Nikki Jewison, Monica Price, Rhosael Ciandre, Becci Lewis, Rachel Morley and Richard Grey.

This one is for you, Mamma.
I love you.

CHAPTER ONE

"YOU can really feel the emotion in this piece, don't you think? The raw state of grief that the artist was in when they created it."

"Oh, absolutely. I can feel the pain mixed with the anger. Look how the red blends into the black, it's like they want to disappear into the void."

Caru looked up from her notebook at the couple in the art gallery, and smiled slightly. She knew the piece they were talking about, and she also knew the artist. What they were saying wasn't even remotely close to the truth.

These situations reminded Caru of English class at school. The teacher would force them to interpret poetry in an attempt to decipher the meaning intended by the poet. But sometimes there was no deeper meaning. Sometimes a poem about rain, really was just about rain.

But if this couple's own interpretation of the artwork encouraged them to buy the piece, she would go along with it, she had her commission to consider after all.

"That piece is an original standalone," she said to the couple, rising up from behind the desk where she had been trying to write an article. "The artist changed mediums after creating it, so there will never be another piece like it." All of which was completely true. Obviously, Caru liked to sell artwork, but it was a policy of hers to always do so with complete honesty. She was terrible at lying.

"Do you know the artist? Are they local?" the woman asked.

Caru noted the woman's delicate gem-encrusted brooch pinned to her perfectly ironed pale pink silk shirt, tucked casually into her perfectly tailored grey skirt.

"Yes I do, and he is local. This piece was created at a pivotal point in his career. He is now focusing on landscapes. His next series is wildly different. This is his final abstract."

The woman nodded, as though she'd had her impeccable taste confirmed. She glanced at the man that Caru assumed was her husband and he nodded slightly. Then she turned back to Caru.

"We'll take it. Could you wrap it and we will collect it on the way back to the car later?"

"Absolutely, come this way and I'll take the payment. It will be all wrapped and ready for you when you get back. We do close at four though." The woman followed Caru to the counter at the back of the gallery.

"We shall be back at three," the woman said, pulling out a large stack of clean, crisp twenties from her Radley handbag. She counted out thirty-five of them and handed them to Caru, who checked them quickly then wrote out a receipt.

"Thank you, I will have it ready for you," she said with

a smile.

The woman nodded and left the gallery with her husband in tow. Caru tucked the money into the safe and wrote the purchase down in the diary. Then she picked up her pen again and tried to concentrate on the article she needed to submit by midnight. She had been trying to get a piece published in *Pressing Matters*, a printing magazine that she loved, but had yet to be successful. The piece needed to be of interest to a wider audience yet be personal at the same time. It was a tricky combination. Caru was trying to explain her love for the art of letterpress printing, but it was really difficult to describe.

She loved composing the words, working out the layouts, the feeling of the sticky ink on the rollers, the satisfying clunk of the impression on the page, and then the finished printed object, with its unique imperfections from the antique type. But conveying that within five hundred words in an eloquent way was evading her. Especially as she also wanted her piece to inspire people who had never tried printing to give it a go.

She scribbled a few more words, then went to the small kitchen to boil the kettle. She could always think more clearly with a cup of coffee. It wasn't as good as the coffee from the little coffee shop on the corner that she visited every morning, but she couldn't afford to get more than one cup a day from there. It was her daily treat.

She got the milk out of the fridge and sniffed it, instantly wishing she hadn't. Her stomach turned and she quickly poured it down the sink and turned on the tap to wash it away. Looked like she would be drinking her coffee black, again. Why couldn't Kevin ever buy more milk? She knew he was a busy guy but surely grabbing some milk didn't take much time? She would have to pick some up in the morning, though she was never usually in town early enough to go shopping before work.

Still muttering to herself, Caru settled back behind the desk, and then quickly shut up and smiled at another browser who entered the gallery. She could tell that they were just looking and not buying, so she left them to it. Normally she would engage in conversation with everyone who walked in the door, but she really did want to finish the article. Besides, she had sold a painting, which made up for the quiet week they'd had so far.

An hour later, she took the abstract acrylic painting down from the wall and wrapped it up carefully in bubble wrap, ready for collection. Then she messaged the artist to see if he had anything else he could bring in to replace it. Kevin didn't like the walls to have bare patches for long. Caru felt that it showed customers that they were selling paintings. Kevin saw it as a wasted opportunity to sell another.

Caru paused by the open door and caught a few notes on the breeze from the busker on the corner. He sat on the doorstep next to the coffee shop every day, singing the usual crowd-pleasing pop songs. But despite the ordinary songs he played, there was something extraordinary in his voice that made her shiver, as though he was speaking directly to her soul.

Which was ridiculous. As ridiculous as the grief the couple had imagined they saw within the abstract. Caru shook her head at her internal musings and went back to the desk to continue her writing.

"Hi, honey, I'm home!" Caru called out to her housemate when she got home later that afternoon. It was a long-standing joke between them, on the account of them both being single and often acting like an old married couple. She took her jacket off and hung it up behind the front door.

"Hi, honey!" Jess called back from her bedroom. "There's parcels in the kitchen!"

"Thanks!"

Caru headed straight to the kitchen of the small flat she and Jess shared. Her heart leapt when she saw the smaller of the two boxes sitting on the counter bearing the *Lyme Bay Press* logo. It was new printing ink, and she already had several designs in mind to use it on. She had hoped it would arrive today.

"More printing stuff?" Jess asked as she came into the kitchen in her signature pink heart fleece pyjama bottoms, turquoise vest top, and penguin slippers.

"Yep," Caru said, grabbing a knife from the block on the counter to open the box. She slit the tape carefully, then opened the box and took the ink tubes out, knowing that she had a late night printing session ahead. She just had to try the new colours straight away.

"I don't get it," Jess said, pouring herself some juice. "I mean, this printing thing has just taken over recently. But before that it was painting, and before that it was photography, and before that..." she frowned, obviously trying to remember what other crafts Caru had become obsessed with.

Caru looked at Jess, still clutching the ink tubes. "What's not to get? I like doing lots of different things." She shrugged. "It's not that weird. Just because you don't have hobbies, doesn't make it wrong."

Jess slugged her juice down in a few gulps. "Hey, I'm not dissing hobbies, I'm just saying that you never seem to stick to any of them for more than five minutes. And you're always saying you have no money and are too busy. I'm just thinking that if you stuck to one thing, you wouldn't spend all your money on new equipment and materials and stuff, and you would also have a bit more time, that's all."

Caru looked down at the box, and pulled out the invoice slip. Her housemate was right, of course. She had spent a lot on her latest interest in printing. But she couldn't help it. She had done a short course at the local library during an art week, and the moment the ink had touched the paper, she'd fallen in love, and she knew she just had to pursue it. Regardless of the cost.

Buying the printing press, the blocks, paper, ink... it had all added up, and her bank account was looking decidedly sadder for it, that much was true.

But the joy it had brought her? That was priceless.

She put the invoice back in the box with the ink and picked up the other package, which contained blank greeting cards and envelopes.

"It's not just for fun though," she said out loud, trying to convince herself as much as her sceptical housemate. "I'm making a whole range of cards to sell at the gallery, and Kevin is really excited about it. So I will make the money back."

"Uh huh," Jess said, now making a cup of tea, her back turned to Caru. "Just try to keep some money for rent? I haven't got enough to cover your arse too."

"You booked your holiday then?"

"Yep, two weeks in the Caribbean, in February." Jess stirred some sugar into her tea and then raised her cup to Caru. "You know, if you were better with your money, you could go on holiday too."

Caru sighed. She hadn't had a holiday for five years. And even then it had been a camping trip to West Wales. It had rained. For the whole week.

Jess left the room, and Caru reboiled the kettle to make her own cup of tea. She would cook some pasta for her dinner later. But right now, all she wanted to do was to print something. The press was calling to her.

She gathered up the packages and headed for her room, picking up her handbag from the hall floor on her way. She nudged the door open with her hip and switched the light on with her shoulder, her hands full.

While the dim energy saver bulb slowly lit the room, she surveyed it with new eyes after her conversation with Jess.

Every surface was covered. Half-finished projects, art materials, unread books, clothes, pens, half-drunk cups of tea...

She saw her knitting project, a blanket for her best friend's baby, still waiting to be resumed by her bed. She saw her unfinished painting still on the small easel, at the back of her desk. In front of that was paper, washi tape and stickers, all waiting to be turned into snail mail and sent to her international penpals.

Caru avoided looking at the box of receipts that she had promised to sort for Kevin, just as she had avoided looking at them for the last three weeks. Why had she volunteered to sort out his accounts for him? She sighed and pushed a few things out of the way, so she could set the parcels down. Her printing table, a makeshift table squeezed into the corner of the room was relatively uncluttered, containing just the necessities for printing. Her beautiful Adana, an old mirror for rolling the ink onto, rollers, chases, some scattered spacers and boxes of metal type.

All waiting to be played with.

Though she hadn't been printing for longer than six months, it brought her such a rush of excitement and joy. When she was carefully composing the type, and trying to line it all up and make sure it stayed in the chase, it felt like a meditative experience, like she was in a whole different world.

"Shit," she muttered, remembering the article she hadn't quite finished. The deadline to be featured in the winter edition of *Pressing Matters* was midnight. She glanced at the clock. It was already nearly seven. Why had she browsed in the shops after work and got the later bus home? She could have been home over an hour before. She grabbed her laptop from underneath the pile of discarded clothing from the morning's mad dash to find something to wear for work, and tapped a key to bring it to life. She took her notebook out of her handbag and flicked to the pages she had filled earlier in the day.

While she waited for her ancient laptop to wake up, she pulled out the boxes of type she wanted to work with. She had an idea for a funny range of cards, and she knew that the metallic purple ink she had just bought would be the perfect colour for them.

When she finally got her writing software to open, she sat on her bed and started typing up her article. She added in her thoughts about printing being meditative, and how it took her into another world. She hoped that it wasn't too 'out there' for the publication. She also added a paragraph about how despite the busyness of her life, printing offered a space for calm.

She hoped that her love of the medium shone through her words, so that other printers wouldn't take offense. Though most of the people she'd encountered in the printing world seemed really cool, she knew that there were many who took it very seriously, and might not agree with her simply figuring it out as she went along. She had read that to become a professional printer, you had to be an apprentice for seven years. Caru hoped that what she lacked in formal training, she made up for in sheer enthusiasm.

It took longer to transcribe her words and shape them into something useable than she had hoped, and by nine o'clock her stomach was growling. She hit the send button and let her breath out in a rush, unaware that she had been holding it. She had no idea why it felt so important to have her piece accepted by the magazine, but she felt like she had finally found a creative community she belonged to, and that being published would somehow prove to everyone that it wouldn't be just another one of her short-lived hobbies.

Caru went to make some pasta, looking longingly at her printing table as she left her cluttered room. She hoped there would still be enough time that night to try out her new inks. Otherwise she was going to find it hard to sleep.

CHAPTER TWO

"THE usual, please."

The barista barely nodded at Caru, and tapped a few buttons on the till screen. It was a good thing they served such great coffee, because the customer service wasn't the best. Caru had been going there every day before work for over a year, and they had still yet to get her name right. Even after spelling it out to them more than a dozen times. It was just four letters, how could it be so difficult?

Caru paid for her order, got her loyalty card stamped, and then moved to the other end of the counter to wait. She was running a bit late that morning, thanks to some crazy traffic. She hoped Kevin wouldn't call the gallery to check she was there exactly at ten. She scrolled through her Instagram feed, which was full of letterpress images and videos, and other crafts. She was just checking out some antique type for sale and was about to hit the buy button when her bank account was saved by the surly barista.

"Order for Carrie!"

Caru slipped her phone into her bag and reached out to pick up the two paper cups. She rolled her eyes at the names on them. "It's C-A-R-U," she muttered, not really loud enough for them to hear. She would have understood them getting it wrong in England, but they were in Wales, there really was no excuse.

She headed out of the coffee shop, and paused to listen to the busker sat on the step for a moment. He had his eyes closed, and was lost in the song he was playing. Caru hated to disturb him when he was clearly in the zone, but she really was going to be very late for work.

"Hey," she said softly, in a quieter part of the song.

He opened his eyes and looked up at her from his perch on the doorstep of the empty shop next to the coffee shop. He smiled and stopped playing.

Caru held out the cup to him.

"Thank you," he said, accepting the tea. "I was wondering where you were today."

Caru chuckled. "I'm running late for work as usual. See you tomorrow?"

He sipped the tea and nodded. "I'll be here. Hope you sell lots of art."

Caru smiled. "That's the plan!" She set off down the cobbled street to the gallery. She pulled her key out and opened the door. Then in a flurry, she put her coffee down, switched the alarm off, got the sign out, switched on all the lights, woke up the computer and before she could sit down, the phone rang.

"Flamingo Fine Art!" she answered chirpily, praying it

wasn't Kevin checking up on her.

It wasn't. She sat in the swivel chair and patiently answered the customer's questions about the upcoming exhibition, and opened up the email on the computer at the same time. By the time the customer had hung up, she found that her coffee was getting cold. She slurped it down as quickly as she could, then when all her gallery duties were taken care of, she started sketching some new card designs, inspired by her late night experiments with her new ink. She hoped that the day would pass quickly so she could try them out.

"I know I said I would be over to visit sooner," Caru said to her friend Laura on the phone as she fumbled in her pocket to find her keys in the dark hallway. The day had dragged by and then she had missed the bus because she needed to buy food. She couldn't afford to keep eating takeaways.

"I know she's three months old already, I have just been so busy, with work and," Caru nearly dropped the phone trying to juggle her bags of shopping while opening the door.

Before she could get the key in the lock, the door opened, and Jess was stood there, dressed up ready to go out. She was wearing a short dark blue dress, impossibly high heels and her favourite red lipstick.

"Date?" Caru mouthed to her housemate, who nodded, grabbed her leather jacket and then went past her down the stairs. How on earth Jess managed to navigate the stairs so confidently whilst walking on miniature stilts was beyond Caru.

Caru went inside, only half-listening to her friend who was still berating her for not going to meet her third child sooner. She didn't seem to notice that Caru hadn't spoken for a few minutes.

She set the bags of food on the kitchen counter and tried not to sigh. She hated disappointing people. She was a self-confessed people pleaser, and loved to make others happy. But sometimes it seemed like an impossible task. There just wasn't enough time in the day or the week or the month to fit everything in. She really did want to visit Laura. She liked babies, and she adored her friend. They had been best friends since school.

But time just seemed to evade her when she was so involved in her projects. It felt as if no one believed that someone who was single with a part-time job and no children could be so busy.

Whereas Caru had no idea how anyone had time to work full time and also take care of spouses and children. She felt like she never stopped, not even in the evenings or the weekends. And she often found it hard to sleep with all the ideas running around her mind for all the things she wanted to create, and all the things she wanted to do.

By the time she hung up, having made several promises to visit as soon as she could, Caru made a mental promise to herself to continue knitting the blanket, so she would at least have a gift to take with her, as she certainly didn't have the spare cash to buy something.

After sorting out Jess's clean washing to be put away, and vacuuming and tidying the living room, Caru had a quick shower, then started making dinner.

In an attempt to be a bit healthier, she made a big

salad and added avocado, nuts, seeds and dried fruit to it, then made herself comfortable in front of the TV to eat. She quickly became engrossed in a show that Kevin had recommended on Netflix, but she made herself pause it to go and get her knitting, so she could feel less guilty about relaxing.

She was four episodes into the series by the time she heard the front door open. The noise jolted her out of her stupor and she looked down at her still hands, the blanket lay forgotten in her lap as she got caught up in the drama on the screen.

Caru set it aside and got up to stretch. She put the kettle on as Jess came into the kitchen.

"How was it?" she asked, setting out two mugs.

"Ugh. Why do I keep doing this to myself? I swear there are just no good men left!" Jess threw herself onto a kitchen stool and kicked off her high heels with a dramatic flair that Caru could never have pulled off.

"Or maybe there are just no good men on Pyre?" Caru suggested, pouring them both some chamomile tea. She needed to sleep soon, and Jess certainly needed a little calm.

"How would you know? You've never even tried the app." Jess was pulling her earrings out and taking off her chunky necklace and rings.

Caru shrugged. "I'm too b-"

"Busy, yeah I know, I know." Jess clunked her final ring on the counter and picked up the cup Caru had given her. "But at some point you need to start looking. Your printing press doesn't give you orgasms does it?"

Caru laughed. "It comes pretty close actually," she admitted. "And it doesn't leave stinky pants everywhere or demand that I cook it dinner." She raised an eyebrow at her friend who was giggling.

"I need a man," her housemate said, her giggles turning into a groan. She sipped the tea, making a face at the heat. Caru took it from her and added some cold water.

"It will happen. You just need to find things you enjoy, and do them. Then you might meet the right guy while doing them." That was her hope, at least. Because when she was actually ready to meet someone, she wanted to have things in common with them.

"You mean like you with your printing? And all the hottie octogenarians you've met through that?" Jess teased. She sipped her tea and nodded at the temperature.

Caru added cold water to her own cup and nodded. "Exactly. I'm gonna to fahh-nd me a sugah printin' daddy who will bequeath his printin' press to me in his will." Her attempt at a southern drawl was terrible, but quite funny, she thought.

Jess groaned again. "The sad thing is, I don't even think you're joking! That would suit you just fine, wouldn't it?"

Caru smiled. "I just don't feel the need to be with a man, I'm quite happy right now. Although," she shook her head and tried to push away the thought. "Never mind."

"What?" Jess demanded, shrugging off her leather jacket and grabbing a blanket from the back of the sofa to wrap around her shoulders. "Who?"

"No one," Caru said, returning to her TV show and abandoned knitting.

"Spill," Jess persisted, following her into the lounge and sitting down on the opposite sofa, an expectant look on her face.

Caru rolled her eyes. "Okay, fine. There's this busker."

"A busker?" Jess cut in. "Are you serious? You have the hots for a homeless man?" Jess's voice was filled with disdain and Caru knew it had been a mistake to say anything.

"He might not be homeless. Just because he busks doesn't mean he doesn't have anywhere to live. But he's there on the corner, every day, and I buy him a cup of tea and we say good morning, and-"

"You buy him a cup of tea? Every morning? Goodness you're soft. It's no wonder you never have any money."

"I know, I know," Caru said, seriously regretting starting the conversation. "I could save the money and go on holiday to the Caribbean instead. But it makes me feel good. And he has a beautiful voice, I love listening to him. Even though he's just playing pop songs, he makes them sound different." She shrugged and sipped her tea. "It's not that I fancy him. I just find him intriguing." She picked up the remote and pressed play.

"Intriguing. Sure. Sounds fascinating."

Caru ignored Jess's sarcastic tone and she didn't look up from her knitting as her housemate left the room, presumably going back to her room to swipe right on her next bad date.

She tried to concentrate on her stitches, but the sound of the busker's voice was running through her mind, and the look in his eyes as she had given him the cup of tea that morning. She was looking forward to seeing him again the next day.

So what if he might be homeless? His presence brought her, and most likely many other people who walked by, some joy. Surely that was all that mattered?

CHAPTER THREE

"EXCUSE me, do you know who makes these cards?"

Caru looked up from her knitting and smiled at the customer who had entered the gallery without her noticing. She carefully put her needles down so she wouldn't drop a stitch and went over to where the woman was browsing through her designs. She had only just put her first range of cards on display that week, and already there had been some interest in them.

"Actually, they're mine," Caru said, feeling a little glow of pride. Could this be her very first sale? She had worked late several nights in a row to get the range done, and she was really pleased with the way they had turned out. She had even printed special packaging for them too.

"Really? They're so beautiful! I don't need any birthday cards right now, but what I do need are some wedding thank you cards. Do you do commissions? I'd love something personal made."

Caru's eyes widened a little and she tried not to show her surprise and glee on her face.

"Oh, of course I take commissions," she said, trying to sound like she got asked all the time. "And I have some time in my schedule right now, when would you need them by?"

"Next week? I appreciate that's a bit short notice, but I'm already late in sending them out."

"No, no, that's fine," Caru reassured her, all the while wondering how she would be able to get them done in less than five days. "Can I take some details?"

She grabbed her notebook from her bag and started jotting down the wording and the number of cards needed, and then did a few quick calculations to work out a price. When she gave the woman the figure, she hoped it wouldn't be too high and put her off.

She needn't have worried, the customer seemed delighted. Which meant she had probably priced it too low, especially as she would have to give Kevin a cut too.

But who cared? She had her first printing commission! She wanted to do a little happy dance, but didn't think it would look very professional. She assured the customer again that it was entirely possible to get the order done in time, and when she left, Caru sat back down behind the counter and started sketching some designs.

Despite her excitement and impatience to get home and get started on the commission, she managed to get through the rest of the day, and even sold a silver ring with rubies and green tourmaline set in it. At four o'clock she gathered her things, switched off all the lights, pulled in the sign, set the alarm and then locked up behind her.

She stepped outside and shivered. It was only the end of September, but autumn was already in full swing. The days were shortening and there was a distinct chill in the air. It seemed like summer was truly over.

When it was warmer and the days were longer, she preferred to walk home, especially as it was often her only form of exercise. But over the winter she usually took the bus home, especially when it was raining or cold, or when she was just too excited to get things done.

Like tonight.

Thanks to her sketches, she already had the design in mind for the thank you cards, and she couldn't wait to test out her idea. She had offered to create three designs for the woman to choose from, which would have been extra work, but the woman had insisted that whatever she created would be perfect. Which was probably a good thing, as in all the excitement, Caru had forgotten to take any contact details.

Caru decided she would try a couple of designs, choose her favourite, then make a set of those, and hope the woman had similar taste. The woman had promised to return for them on Monday morning, and Caru really wanted to impress her.

Caru reached the bus stop just in time to see the bus tail lights go round the corner and she sighed. Looked like she would be walking after all. The next bus wasn't due for another forty-five minutes, and she could be home by then.

As she walked down the high street, she occasionally looked in the windows of the shops she passed. Her favourite charity shop had a gorgeous knitted green cardigan on the mannequin in the window which made her pause.

It wouldn't hurt to look at it, surely?

Half an hour and twenty pounds later, Caru left the shop with a bagful of clothes, including the green cardigan. Clothes shopping in charity shops was a favourite pastime. She always found the best bargains, and her colourful wardrobe was almost entirely made up of second-hand clothing.

She glanced at her phone and figured she might as well get the bus home now, it would be along in ten minutes. She would have to hide the new clothes from Jess before she got home from her late meeting. The last thing Caru needed was another lecture about spending money on things she didn't need. She knew that her latest purchases would become favourites, she had a good feeling about them.

Besides, how could it be wrong to buy such amazing bargains?

Five days later, Caru stared at her nails, wondering why she'd let Jess talk her into having them shaped and polished. At least she'd managed to avoid having huge plastic talons glued on. How would she ever make anything? As it was, she wasn't sure how she would get any printing done without ruining the perfect nail job that Jess's friend Kate had done.

"Nice nails."

Caru looked up at the barista who was waiting for her to step up to the counter and order, and smiled. "Thanks, I don't normally do anything with them."

"I know. The usual?" Her tone wasn't sarcastic, just matter of fact. Considering their lack of interaction, Caru was surprised she had noticed.

"Yes, please."

While waiting for her drinks, Caru inspected her nails again. They felt weird. Jess laughed at her when she said she never painted her nails because she could feel the weight of the polish on her fingertips, but it was true. She wondered how long she would last before picking at the edges.

"Order for Carrie!"

Caru collected her two cups, noting that as usual, her name was spelled wrong. She wouldn't mind so much, but it meant that the busker guy would think that her name was spelled that way.

What did it matter though? She didn't even know what his name was.

Caru was early that morning, so she listened to his singing for a few minutes before handing him the tea.

"Lovely morning," he commented, taking a sip of the scalding liquid.

"It is," Caru agreed. She tried to sip her coffee, but it was still too hot. "My name isn't spelled that way, it's C-A-R-U." Her cheeks reddened slightly, why had she said that? He probably didn't care.

He looked at her name on the cup. "Is that the Welsh spelling?"

Caru nodded. "Yes, it means love." Her blush deepened. Why hadn't she stuck to discussing the weather?

The busker smiled up at her. "That's beautiful."

"Thank you, I, uh, better go."

"Have a great day, Caru."

"You too," Caru said, already walking away, her cheeks burning. She wondered why she couldn't engage in a deeper, more meaningful conversation with him without becoming a mess. Was it nerves because she was so attracted to him? Or was it because she was afraid there was no spark at all?

It was hard to tell.

As she put the sign out and switched on the lights, she thought about her conversation with Jess. Over the last week she had found herself scrutinising the busker's appearance more than usual. Today, he wore threadbare jeans with torn knees, a faded t-shirt with a washed-out cotton shirt and a thick padded plaid jacket over the top. On Friday, he had worn pretty much the same, with a different t-shirt under his shirt.

In short, he looked like a typical musician. He never seemed to have anything other than his guitar and guitar case with him, so she surmised that he wasn't actually homeless. She hoped not, especially as the temperature was now dropping rapidly at night. She had wanted to ask him if he had somewhere to stay, if he had someone who cared about him. If he needed a friend. But she couldn't quite get the words out.

Caru took the box containing the custom thank you cards out of her bag and put them safely in the cupboard under the counter ready for the woman to collect. Caru had spent most of the weekend making them, and she really hoped that the woman liked them, because in order to achieve the effect she had in mind, she'd bought a heavier weight card and it had cost more than she had budgeted for. So she really needed the woman to pay her. Maybe she should have asked for payment up front, or at least half of it. Next time, she would ask for a deposit. And some contact details.

By two o'clock, Caru was feeling quite low. She couldn't believe she had been so stupid as to not even take a deposit. Now she was out of pocket and had wasted a whole weekend making something that would never be used. It wouldn't have been so bad if they had been generic, but they had the bride and groom's first names on them, so there was no way she could sell them to anyone else.

Why was she so trusting?

The very least the woman could have done was let her know she didn't need them. But to simply not pick them up or say anything, well that was just rude.

Caru tried not to berate herself too much, it was an honest mistake to make. One she wouldn't repeat, but it was difficult to silence the voice in her head telling her she was an idiot.

She tried to concentrate on writing, as she had some articles she needed to write for a local magazine she did some occasional freelancing for. But she was too distracted by her thoughts and repeatedly checking the clock and praying that she was wrong about the woman. By closing time, there had been no sign of her, and Caru gave up hope. She left a note for Kevin explaining where the cards were in case the woman came in to collect them the next day when she wouldn't be working, but something in Caru's gut told her that she wouldn't.

Feeling deflated, Caru locked up the gallery and headed down the street, wishing she hadn't promised her neighbour that she would help her bath her dog. He was a big, smelly mutt, and didn't seem to like Caru very much.

But her neighbour was elderly and couldn't lift him into the bath, so Caru had offered to help. Mainly because then she wouldn't have to put up with his smell in the hallway, but also because she couldn't help herself when it came to volunteering to do things she didn't have time to do.

After ten minutes of standing at the bus stop, she was shivering in her thin jacket. The bus was late and the temperature was dropping fast. Could the day possibly get any worse?

The first drop hit her nose. The next six million drops hit her all over.

Apparently, it was possible.

CHAPTER FOUR

CARU bounced gently from side to side as she held her friend's latest addition to the family.

"Goodness she's quite heavy," she commented. Her arms were already tiring, and she had only been holding her for a few minutes.

"She *is* four months old," Laura said pointedly. "She's grown quite a bit."

Caru didn't respond. She couldn't admit that she had delayed her visit so she could finish the blanket, and because she had to wait until payday to have enough money to buy a train ticket. It was too embarrassing. Laura's husband had a great job, so despite their huge mortgage and three children, they always had plenty of money. They didn't have to wait until payday to afford the basics.

After working her fingers into a constant cramp for the last three weeks to get the blanket done, Caru had felt deflated by Laura's reaction to it. She had commented on how nice a colour it was, then set it aside and not mentioned it again. It was now sat forgotten under the wrappings. She hadn't even shown it to Rob, not that he would be likely to appreciate it either.

Caru knew that receiving a lot of gratitude wasn't the point of giving gifts, but some acknowledgment of her effort would have been nice. Maybe she should have just bought something after all. She could have spent the extra time writing articles to make more money instead. She had hoped that the blanket might become a permanent fixture in little Mary's life, as her own baby blanket had been, but it looked like it might never get used at all.

Caru continued bouncing gently on the balls of her feet while little Mary slept in her arms and Laura flitted about the kitchen, simultaneously cooking dinner while fielding questions from toddlers and averting mini disasters as the oldest tried to help with the cooking.

She knew she wouldn't learn from this. She would continue putting too much effort into things that people didn't appreciate or notice, and she would continue to feel disappointed when they didn't react in a way that made her feel good.

Caru could almost hear Jess lecturing her about giving people too much power over how she felt. And she would be right. But that was just who she was. She loved to do things for others, even if they didn't ever return the effort. She didn't know how to be any other way. She didn't want to be any other way. Did she?

Caru sighed quietly. She was probably overreacting. She knew that her friends did appreciate her efforts, but why couldn't she feel it?

Dinner was a noisy and messy affair, and once again, Caru wondered how people managed with small children on a daily basis. Laura's husband was lovely, but he didn't seem to notice the chaos erupting around him as he kept one eye on the football on the TV throughout the meal.

Caru found herself washing up the mountain of dishes and pots and pans at the end of the evening, while Laura tried to get all three kids to settle down to sleep, and Rob snored in front of the movie they'd given up on watching.

As she scrubbed a particularly stubborn bit of food from a pan, she wished she hadn't agreed to stay the night, because she really needed to get some more cards made for the gallery. They had been selling well, and she needed to make sure she kept a healthy stock so she didn't miss out on sales. She'd even had another commission. And although it was a small one, she had priced it better this time, and had asked for half of the price upfront as a deposit. So she had at least learnt from her expensive mistake.

It had seemed too expensive to visit her friend for just a few hours, so to make the most of the train ticket, Caru had agreed to stay over. She had hoped that she and Laura would get some time to chat properly, but the constant interruptions had made maintaining a normal conversation next to impossible.

When the dishes were all done, Caru sat down on the opposite end of the sofa to Rob. He continued to snore, so she picked up the remote and changed the channel until she found an episode she hadn't seen of *Britain's Biggest Hoarders*.

Though it made her feel uncomfortable, it also made her feel at least a little better knowing that she wasn't nearly as bad as the people featured in the programme. At least she could still see her bedroom floor. Well, just about. Besides, she wasn't a hoarder, she didn't keep rubbish. She collected clothes and craft materials. That was completely different.

No matter what anyone said.

Caru stared at her laptop screen and blinked several times, hoping that the number might change if she willed it to hard enough.

But there was no escaping it. She didn't have enough money in her bank account to pay her rent. Shame and fear swirled in her stomach, making it cramp up. How had she managed to do this? She had bought some more supplies to make cards, and she had bought the train ticket, and then there was her food shopping...

Caru scanned through her statement, hoping that maybe there were transactions that weren't hers that she could challenge. But they were all familiar. She noted that there were lots of little purchases that had added up. She hadn't been particularly extravagant with one thing, just spent lots of little amounts. Aside from food, most were on completely unnecessary things. That was the trouble with working in town; she walked past the shops every afternoon. The temptation to buy things was too much. If only she hadn't bought that dress in the charity shop the other day. It was perfect if any weddings came up, but how often did she really get invited to any? It had been a silly purchase. Even if it had fit perfectly.

She felt a twinge of guilt at buying herself clothing

when she had struggled to afford to visit her friend. She thought about the people on the hoarding TV programme. She had judged them for having no control, but maybe she was the one with a problem.

She looked around her room, which was looking even more like a bombsite than usual, thanks to her busy week. Clothes were strewn everywhere, with more in the wash basket than there were hanging up in her wardrobe. She considered some pieces that she didn't wear much. Maybe she could sell some of them on eBay?

Caru sighed. It still wouldn't give her the amount she needed quickly enough. The standing order would be leaving her account in a few days. She pulled out her emergency cash stash from her bedside table drawer, but she knew even without opening it that it wouldn't yield much. She had already pilfered it to pay for the last takeaway. Sure enough, it contained only a few coins and a lone fiver. There was no other option, she would have to ask Kevin for an advance on her wages again, which was embarrassing, even though he always seemed to understand. Maybe if she finally sorted his paperwork for him, he would be more inclined to help her.

Caru put the cash away in the drawer, then closed her laptop and placed it on her desk before flopping onto her bed. She stared up at the ceiling, feeling familiar tears of frustration stinging her eyes.

Why was she so bad with money? Was it just because she spent too much on her creative projects? And on drinks for strangers? And on clothes that she couldn't resist? And on takeaways? Or was it because she wasn't earning enough? She did find it difficult to charge much for her work, or to ask for more money.

Most people her age were earning far more than she was. It didn't help that she only worked part-time at the gallery, and what she earned from her printing she usually ended up reinvesting in more printing equipment and materials.

Once again, she wished she had savings. That she had been more careful with her money over the years. But growing up, the family motto had been – if you have it, spend it. And so she had. But perhaps it was time to rewrite these old mottos and beliefs. She had been estranged from her mum since her teens, after they'd had an argument over her father abandoning them when she was just four years old. Their relationship had never recovered, and just four years ago, she had learned that her mum had died in a car accident. It hadn't surprised her when she discovered that her mum had left everything she owned to a homeless shelter, and had left her nothing. Caru supposed she should just be grateful not to have inherited any debts.

Having no family she could call upon, meant that she had no one to ask for help. Caru was proud of the fact that she had managed to sustain herself despite having no parental support. But it did make times like these trickier to navigate.

What she needed right now was a plan. A plan to ensure she didn't keep messing up her finances.

But in that moment, she was just too overwhelmed and needed to escape. She got up, picked up the box of receipts from her desk and grabbed her fluffiest jumper, slipped it on, then went to the kitchen and made a cup of tea. She then sat on the sofa in the living room and picked up the remote.

As she sorted through the box, putting the papers into neat piles and watching people screaming at each other on the screen, the shame and fear continued to make her stomach clench. She hoped that a couple of hours of doing a mundane task and watching reality shows, where people had worse problems than she did, would calm her down.

It wasn't like it could make her feel much worse.

It had been raining all day, and not a single customer had come through the door of the gallery. Which at least meant it didn't matter that she was wearing her remaining clean black dress a second day, because there was no one there to even notice. She had found it tucked at the back of her wardrobe, having not been worn since her mother's funeral. It was against her normal colourful dress code, but it was the only smart thing that wasn't crumpled up on the floor. She really did need to do some laundry soon.

Caru was going out of her mind with boredom. She had rearranged some sculptures, finished sorting the receipts, dusted and vacuumed, and doodled some new card designs to fill the spaces in the card rack. But the time still dragged by.

Her cards were selling well, and she needed to come up with some new ranges, which was exciting, even though she wondered when she would have the time. She had started knitting a jumper for Jess for Christmas, and some soft toys for Laura's girls. She figured if she didn't start making gifts now, December would arrive before she knew it and she wasn't likely to have spare cash to buy last minute gifts. It was nearly October, so she was already behind.

The rain continued to fall and she bounced up and down in her seat, wishing she had brought her knitting with her. She could have made a sleeve in the time she had wasted pretending to be busy.

Caru sighed. She was feeling a bit grumpy, and wondered if it was hormonal. Because even her cup of coffee that morning hadn't brightened her day. There was a new barista and he was clearly still in training because it hadn't tasted right at all.

Caru wondered if she should stop buying it, and save the money she spent. It added up to quite a bit over the course of a month. But then that would mean stopping buying the cup of tea for the busker guy, and she knew that even the money saved wouldn't make her feel any better.

His smile every morning made it worth every penny. Even though they still hadn't moved beyond light chatter about the weather and what art was selling well in the gallery. She still didn't even know his name. Maybe that's why she was in a bad mood, the rain had kept him away, so she hadn't seen him that morning.

She sighed again and stared at the clock. It was only three, so she had another hour to kill. She couldn't leave early because she really needed every hour of pay. She was determined to try and manage things better so she didn't need another advance on her wages. At least she'd had the money for the cards she'd sold, so that had helped. But no matter how much she wanted to, Caru never seemed to be able to save any money to give her a buffer. Every month was a massive stretch to make it to the end without going into the red or using her 'emergencies only' credit card. She had so far managed to pay off the card each time she had money in her account again, but she was heading towards creating debt and she hated that.

When she was finally able to close up for the day, Caru headed to the bus stop, her hood up and head down against the driving rain. But her flimsy rain coat was of little use against the torrent. She reached the stop the same time as the bus, and climbed onboard, thankful that she didn't have to wait and get even more wet. Though by then, it felt like even her underwear was soaked through.

She sat down four rows from the back and lowered her hood. The bus was mostly empty, only an elderly lady with a trolley sat at the front, and a guy with a leather jacket and a shaved head sat right at the back. Caru put her bag on the seat next to her and then leaned back in the seat. She rested her head on the window that quickly steamed up with her breath, and closed her eyes.

Everything in her body ached. Her back, her shoulders, even her head. Worrying about money and trying to juggle so many balls while still trying to eat well and get some exercise and keep her friends happy, was just proving to be too much. She was completely exhausted. Jess was right, she needed a holiday. But she couldn't imagine being able to afford one in this century.

Caru opened her eyes and watched the shops whizz by and turn into the indistinct blur of trees. She wished that she could stop caring so much. If she didn't love to do so many different things, and try to make others happy, her life would be simpler, easier, with time to rest and relax and go on holidays.

Caru closed her eyes again and began to visualise what

a simpler life might feel like. She smiled at the idea of making enough money to have time off to relax without feeling guilty. The thought of sitting on a beach with a cocktail seemed like bliss. Going out to the cinema with a friend, or having a meal out, without worrying about how much it would cost… She couldn't even remember the last time she'd just sat for a few hours to read a book… She lost herself in her daydream until she nearly fell asleep.

The ringing of the stop bell jolted her and she looked around to see that the bus was now empty and at a standstill at her stop.

She grabbed her bag and jumped up and ran to the front. Her feet slipped around in her sodden shoes, she couldn't wait to get a hot shower.

"Thank you!" she called to the driver, wondering how he had known where she lived, but thankful that she hadn't had to walk any further than necessary in the bad weather.

"May you get all you wish for," he replied with a nod.

Caru nodded back and jumped off, barely taking in his bizarre words. All she was focused on was getting back to her flat through the continued driving rain.

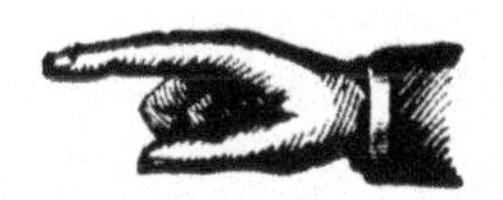

CHAPTER FIVE

THE flat was dark when Caru let herself in. Jess must have been working late again. She closed the door behind her and headed for the kitchen. She was shivering and needed a cup of tea and a shower to warm up. She put the kettle on, and flicked through the post, disappointed that there hadn't been any packages. She had ordered some more paper and it hadn't arrived yet.

Caru made her tea and then went to her room to grab a towel, but when she switched the light on and her eyes adjusted to the dim glow, she nearly dropped her mug in shock.

Her room was empty. Or, near enough empty. The floor and desk were clear, with just a few bits neatly stacked. The bed was made and the wardrobe was closed. The chair was empty. There was no printing table, no press, no books, no knitting projects, no easel, no art supplies, no mountain of stationery, no mess.

All of her possessions were simply… gone.

Her mouth opened and closed and she gasped for air, trying to compute what on earth was going on.

She heard the front door open and she squeaked out her housemate's name.

"What is it?" Jess asked, coming up behind her. Caru stepped into the room and Jess followed, staring at her with concern.

"We've, we've been robbed," Caru gasped.

Jess's eyebrows shot up. "What? Seriously? What have they taken?"

"Everything!" Caru gasped, putting her mug down on a coaster on the desk before she spilled it everywhere.

"Mac? iPad? What?" Jess asked.

Caru frowned. She didn't even own a Mac or an iPad, just an ancient HP laptop. She looked over to the bedside table, and sure enough, there was a MacBook air and an iPad next to it. Jess went over to them and picked them up. "They're here! Did they take anything else?"

Caru scanned the room, and saw that despite the complete lack of creative chaos, it didn't look like it had been ransacked. It just looked... tidy. But why would someone steal all her craft projects but leave expensive gadgets? And how were there expensive gadgets in her room?

Her mind was jumbled and her confusion was obviously showing on her face. She felt sick and scared.

"Are you okay? Come and sit down."

Jess guided her out to the kitchen, and helped her onto a stool at the breakfast bar. She got some chocolate out of the cupboard and handed a piece to Caru, as though she had seen a dementor and the chocolate would fix it.

"What's going on?"

Caru took the square and stared at it, feeling like her whole world had shifted and she genuinely had no idea what was going on. She put the chocolate in her mouth and lifted her shoulders.

"Why did you think we had been burgled?" Jess persisted. "Was the door open?"

Caru let the chocolate slowly melt in her mouth while she tried to formulate a response. Her housemate seemed to think her room was completely normal, that there wasn't anything out of place, despite it looking like it had been torpedoed just that morning. How was that possible?

She looked up at Jess, who had her arms crossed and an expectant look on her face.

"Do I like printing?" she asked.

Jess frowned. "Printing? You have a printer for your computer, is that what you mean?"

Caru shook her head. "No, I mean letterpress printing."

"Not that I know of? I don't even think I know what that is."

Caru swallowed hard. What the hell was going on? "Knitting? Sewing? Art?"

Jess continued to shake her head.

"And my room looks normal to you?"

"Of course. It's as perfectly tidy as always. Though you normally don't leave your shoes out on the floor like that."

Caru began to shiver, and realised that she was still wearing her wet clothes.

"Why don't you get a shower, and I'll make food tonight? It's been ages since we ate a meal together."

Caru nodded. "Or we could get a takeaway?"

Jess laughed. "Takeaway? We never eat takeaways.

They're expensive and unhealthy."

Caru's eyes widened slightly but she said nothing. They didn't eat takeaways? Since when? They had one at least three or four times a week. Something was definitely not right.

She got off the stool and headed for her room. She took the towel off the hook on the back of the door and headed to the bathroom, all the while trying to figure out what was going on. Had she entered some kind of alternate reality? Or hit her head and started hallucinating?

She turned the shower on and stripped off, now shivering uncontrollably. A thought occurred to her and her shivering abruptly halted.

Was she dead? Had the bus crashed? Was she in a coma? Or in heaven?

The plots of a thousand movies ran through her mind as she got under the stream of hot water.

She really hoped she wasn't dead. Kevin would be so annoyed if she missed work.

A giggle escaped from her lips at the ridiculous thought. She concentrated on washing her hair and tried to release the mess in her mind.

She would need all her wits to be able to solve this bizarre situation.

Afraid of freaking Jess out too much, Caru had gone to bed straight after dinner, which was a really tasty stirfry with rice noodles. It seemed Jess was a great cook. She wondered if she would magically have cooking skills now too.

After a fitful night of weird dreams, she woke up, having forgotten about the previous evening's strange events, and found herself shocked by the state of her room once again.

The perfectly immaculate state of her room, that was.

As she scanned the room, her eyes slowly came into focus after waking suddenly. Her gaze rested on her MacBook, and she reached out for it slowly, not daring to believe it was really hers.

She opened it up, and the bright screen lit up the room in the dim autumnal morning light.

It required a password to access it, and without thinking Caru tapped in her usual password, slightly amazed when it worked. Immediately, emails began pinging through, and she muted the sound. She opened her inbox and there was the usual junk mail, but there were also emails from a travel magazine that she loved. She scanned through them, her eyes widening. It would seem that she wrote for the magazine…

She looked up at her neat bookcase, and spied a small stack of the magazine there. She set the Mac aside, and got up to grab the copies off the shelf. She got back under the covers and started thumbing through them. It didn't take long to find an article that bore her name at the bottom. She read it quickly, and though she could hear her own voice, she had no recollection of having written it, or indeed of having ever visited the location the article was about. But there she was, in one of the pictures, looking very happy outside a tiny bakery on the Greek island.

Surely this was all just a dream?

Her alarm sounded. She turned it off and got up. She didn't want to be late for work. Although at this point she wasn't even sure if she worked at the gallery or not.

Fear gripped her again, and she tried to shake it off. But it was difficult when nothing felt real anymore. She took several slow, deep breaths to try and calm down before getting ready to leave.

Caru packed her MacBook along with her notebook into her handbag, not really sure why, but feeling that it was important to have it with her. Getting dressed was easy, she literally only had a handful of items in her wardrobe, and they all matched. Probably because they were all mostly black. She hung her black dress from the day before back in her wardrobe because for some reason it bothered her to leave it on the back of her chair. Then she headed for the kitchen and had a quick bowl of cereal before dashing to the door. She was about to leave when Jess called out from her room.

"Hey, are you okay?"

"Yeah," Caru called back. "Just don't want to be late."

"Me too, could I hitch a ride?"

Caru frowned. "A ride?"

Jess came out of her room, still shoving her arm in her jacket sleeve. "Yeah, it's on your way so it shouldn't make you late. My car is in the garage and Carol can't pick me up." She rolled her eyes. "Some kind of pet emergency."

When Caru continued to look at her blankly, Jess snapped her fingers.

"Sorry, I forgot to say, your keys are here, John dropped them off with the car late last night, after you'd gone to bed."

Caru looked down at the keys Jess handed her, complete with a fluffy pink pompom keyring attached. She wondered who John was.

"Um, sure, yeah, I can give you a ride," she said finally, attaching her work and house keys to the pompom.

Jess grinned. "Thanks, I owe you."

They went down the stairs and headed out of the huge double doors, and Caru halted suddenly when she saw the beautiful pink Mini Cooper in one of the parking spots for their flat. It even had a personalised number plate.

CARU 1

"Come on, I thought you didn't want to be late," Jess said, heading for the passenger door.

Caru snapped out of her daze and pressed the button on the fob to open the door. Jess stepped in and Caru hurried to the driver's side, hoping that she would remember what to do. She hadn't driven a car in a couple of years as her last one didn't pass the MOT and she hadn't had the money to replace it.

"So, um, where do you want me to drop you off?"

"On the corner of the high street is probably easiest," Jess replied, not noticing that Caru was quickly trying to work out all the controls. The car was much newer than her last heap of junk, and had way more buttons and levers.

She got the car started and carefully backed up and turned around in the wide driveway. Then she headed down the road, glad that she at least knew where Jess wanted to be dropped off, even if she now wasn't entirely sure where she worked herself. Surely she couldn't afford such a beautiful new car with her meagre part-time wage? And she no longer did any printing, or other arts and crafts. So where did the money come from?

Jess chattered away about nothing in particular, she had clearly forgotten all about Caru's weird breakdown the night before, or maybe she was just avoiding mentioning it for fear of setting her off again.

She dropped her housemate off on the corner, then headed to the car park closest to the gallery, assuming that's where she would park for work.

She got out of the car and bought a ticket at the machine. Glancing at her watch, she knew she had at least ten minutes, so she decided to grab her usual coffee. Maybe a few minutes of listening to the busker would help calm her racing mind.

The busker wasn't on the corner when Caru walked up the street, but no doubt he would be along at any moment. Sometimes, she wondered if he timed his arrival to coincide with her going to work. But that seemed ridiculous. Caru stepped into the coffee shop and was greeted with a huge, although possibly not very genuine, smile from the usual barista.

"The usual?" she chirped.

Caru nodded and tapped her card on the machine. She couldn't find her loyalty card in her wallet so she started a new one. Then she moved to the end of the counter to wait for her order. She scrolled through Instagram on her phone, noting that she appeared to mainly follow travel bloggers and magazines, and food blogs, but hardly any creative ones. She looked at her own feed, and found photos of all the places she'd apparently visited.

"Order for Caru!"

Caru looked up from her phone and reached out for her coffee, noticing that for the first time ever, they had spelled her name right. She smiled and looked at the barista. "Thank you!"

The barista nodded and moved away to make more orders.

"Hang on," Caru said, "I've got a tea, too?"

The barista turned back and shook her head. "No, you ordered a coffee. Just like you do every day."

Caru frowned. "I don't normally get a tea? I get it for the busker who sits next door, every morning."

"You mean Charlie? Didn't you hear? It was in the news."

"Hear what?" Caru asked, pleased to finally know his name but feeling anxious as to why he would be in the news.

"He committed suicide, about a month ago."

Caru felt like her heart had stopped. "But he was there just..." she was going to say 'the day before yesterday' but knew that it would sound insane.

"Sorry," the barista said, not sounding particularly sorry. "Didn't know you knew him."

"I didn't," Caru whispered, hot tears running down her face, more than likely ruining the expensive mascara she had found in her makeup case and had carefully applied that morning.

"Oh, well, have a good day," the barista said awkwardly before moving onto the next order.

Aware that she had been dismissed, Caru left the coffee shop and only made it to the doorstep on the corner where the busker – Charlie, she reminded herself – used to sit.

She sat down on the cold concrete step and stared blindly at the people rushing by her.

Charlie was dead. It was weird, finally learning his name now that he was gone. But how could he have died a month ago? And how come she had a brand new car, and wrote for a travel magazine, and had no artistic hobbies?

Surely this had to be a weirdly realistic dream that she would wake up from. But the concrete underneath her felt too cold to be a figment of her imagination.

Caru breathed in deeply and dug in her pocket for a tissue. She blew her nose and stood up, a little unsteady on her feet. She pulled out her phone to check the time, and realised she was going to be late.

Caru walked as fast as she could to the cobbled lane without spilling her coffee, which was still too hot to drink, and reached the gallery door just as Kevin did.

"Kevin! I'm so sorry I'm late! I just had some bad news and it delayed me a little." She felt a spike of guilt for using Charlie as an excuse, but she hated the look in Kevin's eyes when he caught her turning up late. Which to be fair, did happen a lot.

Kevin finished unlocking the gallery door and looked up at her, confusion on his face.

"I'm sorry, do we have a meeting?" he asked, going into the gallery and switching on the lights.

She followed him in. "No, it's my day to work? We swapped days, remember?"

Kevin picked up the sign and put it outside, then came back in, still frowning at her.

"Work? I don't know what you mean. I work here. This is my gallery. Who did you say you were?"

Caru laughed. "Kevin are you having a senior moment? Because you're too young for that. It's me, Caru? Your indentured slave, friend and card maker?" She gestured to where her cards were displayed on a stand. Only to find there was no stand, and no cards.

Because, of course, she had no printing press and didn't do anything creative.

Because apparently, she was no longer in Kansas.

"Oh," she said. "So, you don't know me?" Tears were beginning to fill her eyes again. How could she never have met Kevin? They'd been friends for years.

"No, sorry sweetheart, I don't. And I do have a meeting in five minutes, so..."

Caru nodded. "Sorry, of course, um, sorry to bother you." She backed up, nearly knocking a sculpture off its plinth. She righted it and left the gallery quickly, not wanting Kevin to see the tears now streaming down her face.

What was she supposed to do now? She obviously worked somewhere nearby, or Jess wouldn't have asked for a lift. But how was she meant to work out where? Perhaps she could search through her emails for some clues.

With that thought, her phone began to vibrate. She pulled it out, it said 'Time Traveller' on the screen.

Thinking that things couldn't possibly get any weirder, she answered the call.

"Yes?"

"Where the hell are you?" the voice demanded.

"Um, outside Flamingo Fine Art?"

"You need to get here as soon as you can. That couple are arriving any minute and you're the only one who can deal with them!"

"Okay, I'll be there as soon as I can," Caru said, already googling Time Traveller and her current location.

"Please hurry!"

The call cut off, and Google pointed out a location just five minutes' walk away, down a side road that Caru almost never frequented. She sipped some of her coffee and set off, wondering what she would find.

CHAPTER SIX

"TIME Traveller Agency! How may I help you?"

Caru stepped through the door into the tiny space and looked around. There were colourful travel posters adorning the walls, a large potted plant in the corner and two desks with chairs in front of them. At one of the desks, there was a young redheaded woman on the phone, who started gesturing at her frantically while calmly answering the query.

Caru stood rooted to the spot by the front door, unsure what to do.

The redhead rolled her eyes at her, and continued talking, obviously trying to wrap up the conversation quickly. When she got off the phone she looked up at Caru and frowned.

"What's wrong? You need to get ready. The Smiths will be here in the next twenty minutes, and you need to be prepared. You know how pedantic they are."

Caru looked at the other desk and saw that it had a mug on it that looked very much like her favourite one. "Um, I, uh, just had some bad news this morning, and it's um, it's..."

"Bad news?" The redhead got up out of her seat. "Shall I put the kettle on?"

Caru nodded. "Yes, please." She went over to the desk, and put her bag down on the chair. She took off her coat and the redhead grabbed it from her on the way to the kitchen, and hung it up on the hook for her.

"Oh, thanks," Caru said. She pulled her MacBook out of her bag and set it on the desk. How was she going to meet with a couple she didn't know? And talk about what? Their travel plans? Clearly she worked as a travel agent in this weird reality she now found herself in, but she had no idea how to be a travel agent.

The redhead placed the hot drink on the desk next to the half-drunk cup of coffee that Caru had bought.

"I don't know why you insist on buying a coffee every morning, when we have a perfectly good coffee machine here." The redhead settled back behind her desk and looked at Caru expectantly. "So, what was the bad news? Are you okay?"

Caru sat down at her own desk and slurped a bit of lukewarm coffee from the paper cup before answering. "I found out that someone I sort of knew had died. I was just shocked. I hadn't seen them that long ago and I hadn't heard about their death."

"Oh that's terrible. How did they die?"

"Suicide," Caru said. She opened her MacBook and tapped in her password. "Um, do you think it's possible to reschedule the meeting with the uh, Smiths?"

At that moment, the door opened and let in a blast of cold air.

"Too late," the redhead muttered, getting up and going to greet the couple.

Caru's heart began to race. How was she going to pull this off? She opened a file on her desktop labelled 'Work' and then opened another folder labelled "TTA". She was hoping to find some clues in there to help her.

"Caru!" the lady said, "Good to see you again, I hope we can get everything sorted today?"

"Um, yes, of course, why don't you both sit down, and I'll find my notes."

The redhead took their coats and said she would get them a cup of coffee. They settled themselves on the two chairs in front of her desk while Caru clicked on a file with their name on it, and found a word document. She opened it and quickly scanned it.

"So, you want to finalise the details for your trip to Finland?"

"Yes, we have a few more things we want to add to the itinerary, which might mean a slight change in hotels, but we're pretty sure that we have figured out everything we want to see now."

"Excellent, well why don't you tell me the changes and additions, and then I will sort it all out and then email it all to you?" Caru held her breath, hoping that it would satisfy them, and that she wouldn't have to work out how to make all the bookings right in front of them.

"Sounds perfect," the woman said. "What about payment?"

"We can take that over the phone," Caru said, having no idea if that were true.

"Great, well, let's get started." Mrs Smith pulled out a notebook from her handbag and Caru took a sip of her coffee. Her redheaded colleague put two mugs in front of the couple, then went back to her desk.

Caru prayed that she could fool the couple into thinking she had any idea of what she was doing, and wondered how she could explain to her colleague that she needed help. Maybe she could say she'd hit her head and had temporary amnesia?

Mrs Smith began to talk and she forced herself to focus and take notes, convincing herself that she could sort it all out later.

Becky, the redhead, had seemed thrilled when Caru had asked her for help with booking the trip for the Smiths, so Caru didn't even give a reason why she needed her help.

Caru vaguely wondered why Becky kept making them coffee and went out to get their regular lunch order, and seemed pleased to be asked to do things. Surely they were equals? It was a little strange how she deferred to her, was Caru her supervisor or something? It was when she left to get their lunch that Caru had a quick glance at her computer screen to look for her name.

The door opened while Caru was still nibbling on her baguette – cheese and onion, her favourite, at least some things were the same – and she looked up to see the postman.

She smiled at him and he handed her a bundle of envelopes and smiled back.

She was wondering if she should open the mail, or

if the boss did that, when she noticed that the top one was addressed to her. And underneath her name, it said 'Director'.

Her eyes widened. Was the travel agency her business? Did she write for an amazing travel magazine *and* have her own travel company?

She was sure she was dreaming. How was it possible that all her childhood dreams had come true? She had given up on her dream of travelling the world and owning her own company when she was about ten years old. Yet apparently, in this world, it had actually happened.

Caru opened the envelope, which was an electricity bill, and her eyes widened. Six hundred pounds? Her heart rate quickened and her stomach clenched. She couldn't even pay her rent this month, how on earth was she going to pay this?

She opened the rest of the envelopes, most were travel brochures but there was another bill. This one was the rent for the agency premises, which was fifteen hundred pounds.

She was definitely getting heart palpitations now.

Becky set another fresh cup of coffee in front of her and Caru smiled up at her colleague. Or was she her employee?

"Do you want me to take care of the bills?" Becky asked, pointing to the papers in Caru's sweaty hand.

"Um, yeah, that would be great, um, do you have all the details?"

"Of course, you gave them to me last week?"

"Oh yeah," Caru handed over the letters. "I forgot."

"You really are a bit unsteady today," Becky remarked. "Do you want to take the rest of the afternoon off? I can field the calls and take any bookings. It was only the Smiths that I couldn't have handled, we don't have any more meetings booked."

Despite her fear of her dwindling bank balance, and worrying over where Becky was getting the funds to pay the bills, Caru knew that she had winged it long enough today, and could do with a time out.

"Yes, actually, I think I need some time. The bad news this morning did kind of knock me a little, I don't think I realised how much." Caru felt guilty again for using Charlie's death as an excuse, especially when she hadn't even thought about him for the last few hours, but she also really needed to escape.

"Um, you have my number if you need anything," she said, gathering her things into her bag and slipping her coat on.

"Of course, don't worry. I will get in touch if there's anything urgent. You go and relax for a bit."

"Thank you, Becky," Caru said, heading for the door. "See you tomorrow?"

If she hadn't slipped back into her old reality, or woken up from her coma by then.

"Yep, see you in the morning. Maybe on time?" Becky teased.

Caru blushed. "Yes, of course."

She left the agency before she could say anything else that might trip her up. She was halfway down the high street, heading for the bus stop, before she remembered that she had a car parked at the top of town in the opposite direction.

"Shit," she muttered, doing a sudden about turn and nearly knocking over the guy behind her.

"Sorry,' she said, as he stumbled backwards.

"No problem," he replied, stepping around her and carrying on.

She hurried up the high street, pausing only for a moment at the corner where Charlie used to sit and sing.

For all of the amazing things that there were in this reality, there were some things she wished could be different. She wondered why he had committed suicide, if he had any family, and if anyone had actually mourned his death.

A tear slid down her cheek as she hurried to the carpark, glad that she would at least be home long before Jess and would have a few hours to have a good cry then try to work out what was going on. If that was even possible.

CHAPTER SEVEN

"WOW, what's all this?"

Caru jumped at the sound of Jess's voice, and spun around to see her housemate trying to read her scribbles all over the large whiteboard in the kitchen.

"Oh, um, nothing, I just needed to figure something out, and needed a big space." Caru put the lid on the pen and put it on the side, she hoped her scrawl wasn't legible enough for Jess to understand.

"New life plan?" Jess asked. "Aren't things going well at the agency? You're not usually home so early, and you've been back early twice in a row now." Jess dumped her handbag on the counter and kicked off her high heels.

"I wasn't feeling well today. I, uh, found out someone I knew had died, and I just couldn't concentrate." Guilt gripped her yet again, but Charlie's death was helping to hide her odd behaviour. She sent him a silent thanks and hoped he wouldn't mind.

"Oh shit, I'm sorry, hon. I'll put the kettle on, do you want to talk about it?"

Jess picked up the kettle and filled it up while Caru grabbed some kitchen towel and began wiping her scribbles out. She didn't want her housemate to think she had completely lost the plot.

When the board was clean again, she threw the paper in the recycling bin and sat on a stool and took the cup of tea offered. "No, it's okay, I didn't really know him, it was just a shock because I hadn't realised." Charlie's smile and the way his eyes lit up every morning when she gave him a cup of tea flashed through her mind and her throat tightened. She hadn't really known him. But she had wanted to. His voice was so soulful, he was so talented.

"I'm here if you need to chat about it. Was it someone you knew through work?" Jess grabbed the biscuit tin, pulled out a chocolate cookie and dunked it in her tea. She pushed the tin toward Caru, who shook her head.

Caru sipped her tea. "No, it was someone in town, just a passing acquaintance."

"It's still a shock though, were they young?"

Caru loved that her housemate was concerned, but all she really wanted to do was retreat to her room because her mind was whirling and it was difficult to maintain a conversation. "Yeah, they were."

Jess could obviously sense that she wasn't going to get much more information out of her, because she glanced up at the clock. "I need to get ready, but if you need me, I can cancel."

"Another date?" Caru hoped the relief wasn't too evident in her voice. She was glad to have the flat to herself for the evening, she still had more to work out.

Jess smiled. "I'm hoping this one's a good one."

Caru smiled back. "I hope so too. You deserve to find a good one. Go and have fun, I'll be fine." Already Caru's mind was back on working out what was going on.

So far, her theories ranged from accidentally slipping into an alternate reality, to being dead and in some kind of afterlife underworld, to her favourite so far – being in a coma and having a very weird dream.

Caru waited until Jess had left the flat for her date before hopping off the stool to go back to the whiteboard.

She started to write down all the things that were different to her previous life, and after a moment, her hand paused mid-air when a thought occurred to her.

Why was she so bothered that her life had changed? So far, apart from Charlie's death, everything was amazing. She had everything she'd ever wanted. Her own business, a new car, a regular writing gig with a travel magazine, and apparently lots of actual travel too.

She put the pen down. What else would have changed? Caru picked up her phone and noticed the app for her bank on the home screen. She needed to check that she had enough for the rent that was due in a week. So she logged in, and even though the figure that popped up in her current account was a surprise, it wasn't much of a shock that she would have more money now. After all, she had no hobbies to spend her cash on, and apparently never ate takeaways.

She scrolled through the transactions and noted that they were all practical purchases. Mostly fuel and food, and occasional clothing. She also noticed there were regular payments to a building society account.

She frowned. Did she have a savings account in

this world? She'd never had a savings account before. There was never enough money to last her through the month, let alone put anything by, the only spare she had was the emergency cash hidden in her room. But there were definitely regular payments going out, that were a substantial amount.

She went to her room, and surveyed the very neat desk. Would she still throw everything into one box like she used to? Surely not. She opened the desk drawers and found everything neatly sorted in each. In the deepest one, she found an accordion file. She pulled it out, and found all her paperwork, her passport, and a sheaf of papers with the building society logo on them. She flicked through her passport first, amazed at how worn it looked. There were stamps covering the pages, some of them to places she'd never even heard of. She hadn't just travelled a little in this life, she had travelled a lot. It was a shame she couldn't remember any of it.

Caru put the passport away and picked up the building society statement with the latest date on it. Her eyes widened and a small gasp escaped. She sat down heavily on her desk chair and stared at the sum on the page, in black and white, clear as day.

Forty-nine thousand, four hundred and fifty two pounds.

She looked at the top of the page, and sure enough, there was her name and address. It really was hers.

This was the result of having no hobbies? Of doing nothing creative? Or at least nothing creative that required expensive equipment and materials?

Caru rifled through the papers to find the oldest statement, and saw that she had started the savings account fifteen years earlier with a lump sum of five thousand pounds. She looked at the date and thought back. It had been her inheritance from her gran, and in her reality, she had spent it on a banger of a car, which had cost a fortune to keep fixing, and books, and art supplies, and various random things that she hadn't kept very long. But in this reality, she had saved it, and continued saving, and now had more than enough money to put a deposit on a house.

She sighed. That was her ultimate dream. To buy her own house. A small cottage with a wood burner, and a little studio to make things in...

She swivelled in the chair to look at the empty corner of her room that should have been home to her printing press.

If she bought a house now she wouldn't need a studio because she didn't make anything. She had yet to find evidence of a single creative hobby.

Caru sighed. How had her life ended up so differently? Something must have happened in her past that had changed things. And why hadn't she already bought a house? The sum sitting in her account was enough to put down a substantial deposit – had she hesitated because she didn't want to leave Jess and live by herself? Or was there another reason?

She rifled through the accordion file, and saw mostly the same paperwork that she had in her other life, just in a neater order. But she frowned when she found an unfamiliar bundle of letters. They were addressed to her, and the post office stamp was dated twenty-five years before, when she would have been just seven years old.

She pulled out the top letter from the bundle, sure that

she vaguely recognised the handwriting, but absolutely certain that she had never seen them before.

'My Dearest Caru,

Thank you from the very bottom of my heart for your letter, I shall be forever grateful to your teacher for suggesting that you write it as an exercise for Valentine's Day. What better time is there to receive a letter from your child who was born on such a beautiful date?

I must first apologise for my absence from your life. I want you to know that it is absolutely not your fault. It is mine. And it is inexcusable. There really are no reasons good enough to not be there for you right now, and my heart breaks that I cannot explain to you why I am not.

I want to impress upon you that you were borne of love, that you were wanted, that you were loved and appreciated. And that you still are, today, tomorrow and every day. You are incredible. I knew that from the moment I first held you.

You can do anything. You can be anything. The possibilities are endless and they are all available to you.

I believe in you. I love you. I hope to hear from you soon.

Much love always,

Dad."

Tears were streaming down Caru's face as she read words that she had never seen before, written by a man she had no memory of. She was only four when he'd left, and her mother never spoke of him. She had asked so many times but had got nowhere. She tried to remember her teacher setting an exercise to write to her father, but couldn't recall one. Had she been ill that day in her other reality? Were these letters the key? Was this why her whole life was different?

She wiped her eyes with her sleeve and pulled out another letter. She had obviously written to her father many times, and every time his replies repeated the same things. That she was amazing, that she could do anything. She found one that told her to save her money so she could buy her own home and build a safe place for her family. She looked up from that letter to glance at the building society statement.

"I did it, Dad. I did it," she whispered. It felt weird to even say the word out loud.

She wondered if her relationship with her mother had been better in this life, if their argument had never happened. Perhaps they had been close before she had passed away?

Caru's eyes widened. What if her mother was still alive? What if she hadn't been in the accident?

She grabbed her phone and scrolled through the contacts. There was no listing for 'Mum' or for her mother's name. But how could she tell for certain?

She tapped on the Google app and typed in some details from the accident. Her heart fell when she found the article that had been released in the local paper after her mum's death. So that had been the same at least.

Caru hoped that maybe they'd had a better relationship, but in all likelihood, they had probably been just as estranged.

She set the letters from her dad to one side, and looked through the rest of the notecards and letters in the file. She found a postcard from her mum, from a trip to Gran

Canaria. She scanned the brief note and frowned. She picked up her dad's letter and compared the handwriting.

They were the same.

That was why the writing had looked familiar. Her mum had written them. Of course she had, why would a man who had abandoned his wife and child be so loving, so encouraging? Her mum had obviously wanted her to feel loved, and so had decided to write the letters, pretending to be her father.

Tears began to fall again, and her heart ached for her mother who had raised her alone, yet still tried to fill the role of both parents.

Considering the possible impact these words had had on her life, her mother had given her the most beautiful gift, and yet she would never know.

The next morning, Caru woke up at seven-thirty, got up, showered, had two cups of coffee, and was dressed and out of the door by eight-thirty. She hadn't seen Jess after her date the night before, so it must have gone well.

She got in the Mini and put her bag on the passenger seat, then applied more lip-gloss using the rear-view mirror. She was halfway to work before she realised that she hadn't even thought about her morning routine, it had seemed perfectly natural and normal.

But this wasn't normal.

Or was it?

As she pulled into the car park near her travel agency, and got out of the car, a thought suddenly struck her.

Had her old life been the dream? Was this actually her

real life?

She really wished she could talk to someone about it, but she knew she sounded certifiable. She remembered the bundle of letters she'd found, and nodded to herself as an idea formed.

"Good morning!" Becky sang as Caru stepped through the door. At least her employee was there before her. There seemed to be an alarm system on the door and Caru wouldn't have had a clue how to turn it off. She would look for the instructions later, just in case.

"How are you feeling today?" Becky asked as she placed a cup of coffee on Caru's desk. Caru pulled off her coat and sat down. Becky took her coat and hung it up for her.

"I'm good," Caru replied. "Let's get the Smith booking all confirmed, because then I would like to get started on the spring brochure. I know it's not the end of the year yet, but you know I like to get a head start on these things."

Becky nodded and immediately set to work on her computer, and Caru frowned.

Where had that come from? Spring brochure? She didn't even know they made their own brochures.

She opened her laptop and picked up her mug. She hadn't felt like going near the coffee shop that morning. It seemed easier to avoid the place where she could still see Charlie sitting on the step, his eyes closed as he played his guitar and sang.

She shook the memory from her mind and focused on her laptop screen. She found that if she didn't think too much, what needed to be done came quite easily and naturally to her, as though she had been doing it for a long time. So somewhere in her subconscious was everything she needed to be able to survive in this odd reality. Which made her wonder again if it really was her old life that was the dream.

The day flew by and aside from a couple of things that she had no memory or knowledge of, she got by without too much trouble. At least Becky was no longer looking at her strangely. By the time she left the office, leaving Becky to set the alarm and lock up, she was feeling quite confident that she could handle anything that was thrown at her. But just in case, there was somewhere she needed to visit before going home.

After a few wrong turns, Caru finally arrived at the cemetery. She parked and then headed down the path, her feet guiding her, even though in her old reality she had only ever visited twice after the funeral.

Without any trouble at all, which was surprising after getting lost driving here, Caru found herself standing in front of her mother's grave. The stone was more ornate than she remembered, and there were fresh flowers there. It was clearly cared for and well-attended, and tears sprang to her eyes again.

Feeling slightly foolish, and bad for not bringing more flowers, she sank to the grass and sat cross-legged, like she had as a child.

"Hey, Mum," she said softly. She glanced around to check no one was within earshot, feeling a bit silly for talking to a stone. But she hoped that wherever her mother was, she could hear her.

"I know what you did. I know that you wrote me those letters, not my dad, and I want to say thank you. I think they are why I have everything I want. Because in my other world, I didn't. I was too busy trying to keep everyone else happy…" Her voice trailed off. "Was that it?" she wondered out loud. "Was I so desperate for love, in whatever form I could find, that I became a people pleaser? Or that I tried to somehow create, or make the love I needed through my crafts?"

She sighed. "I don't suppose I will ever know. But it does feel like unconditional love from my father would have created this… stability that I have now. This life where I have a business, a car, savings, and a sense of order and peace." She chuckled a little. "My other life was filled with chaos and disorder and struggle." She thought about her disastrous attempts to date in the past. "And men who didn't have the capacity to love me in the way I desperately needed."

Seeing her old life through the lens of this life was eye-opening. She had craved connection and love, because she hadn't found it within herself.

How could she have, when the two people in the whole world who had a duty to love her unconditionally, had not?

"I hope we had a good relationship in this life, Mum. I hope that we talked and laughed, and I was able to appreciate all that you did for me. Because you gave me everything." Her voice cracked. "You gave me so many gifts. So much love. And I can see it all now." She bowed her head, and her tears fell to the soft grass. "I love you, Mum. I hope you are happy wherever you are, and I hope you stay with me as I try my best to work out what on earth is going on. Because I feel like I'm going to need some support."

She wiped her face with the sleeve of her black coat and uncrossed her legs, feeling a bit cold and stiff. The light was fading fast and a breeze picked up suddenly through the ornamental trees.

"I'll see you soon, Mum. Caru ti."

She walked back to her car, feeling lighter. She hadn't realised how big a grudge she had held against her parents, and how much that could have affected her whole life. The decisions she had made, the paths she had taken.

She began to hope that the old life really had been the dream, because she knew now, that this was the path she wanted to be on.

CHAPTER EIGHT

THE flat was dark when Caru arrived home half an hour later, and she wondered if Jess had even come home yet. She hadn't sent an SOS so hopefully she was still alive after her latest Pyre adventure. Caru took off her coat and went to hang it in her room. She caught the scent of something delicious coming from the kitchen and frowned. Why would Jess have left something cooking while she wasn't in? She was sure she hadn't seen her car in the driveway, but then, it was dark outside.

She put her bag down and made her way down the dark hallway to the kitchen, and slowly pushed the door open. The smell got stronger and she was surprised to see the kitchen and the lounge lit only by dozens of tealights in jars dotted around.

"Jess?" she called out.

"No, it's me," a voice called from the sofa.

Caru squinted in the candlelight as the figure stood

up and headed over. When his features became a little clearer, her heart skipped a beat. Goodness, Jess had hit the jackpot.

"I'm so sorry," she said, smiling involuntarily. "I don't think Jess is here."

He smiled and moved closer. "I know she isn't. I asked her to stay at Kate's so we could have the place to ourselves."

He wrapped his arms around her waist and leaned down to kiss her. Without thinking, she lifted herself up onto tiptoes to meet his lips.

When they parted, she blinked. He seemed so familiar, and yet, she had never met him before. Was he her boyfriend? He was staring at her intently and she could feel a blush creeping into her cheeks. Thank goodness it was so dimly lit in there.

"I'm sorry I was confused, I just wasn't expecting you," Caru said, hoping that it was the right thing to say.

"I know, I asked to be let go a couple of days early. I figured I needed to do something big to make up for being off grid and unable to call you for days. Especially when I saw that you stopped leaving voicemails two days ago. I thought you must be really pissed with me."

Caru shook her head and accepted the glass of red wine he had poured, her mind whirling.

"No, I've just had a very hectic few days, that's all."

He reached for her again and kissed her. "Thank goodness. Does that mean I'm forgiven?"

"Of course," Caru said, breathing in his musky scent. "Forgiven." She would have said anything if it meant she got to kiss him again. Even if he was a complete stranger to her in that moment.

He grinned and went to check on the food in the oven. She breathed in the scent of lasagne and sighed. "That smells like heaven," she said.

"Don't worry, I know you're only with me for my cooking," he teased. He set to work chopping garlic.

"Garlic bread too?" Caru asked, her stomach growling suddenly.

"Of course, it's my speciality, mia cara."

Caru laughed. "You're not Italian," she sipped her wine, wondering if she'd made a huge error. "Are you?"

The man chuckled and picked up his wine. "Only in the bedroom," he replied with a wink.

Caru swallowed her mouthful of wine too quickly and nearly choked.

He put his glass down and patted her on the back. "Do you need some water?"

She shook her head and cleared her throat. "No, I'm fine. Um, I think I might just shower, if there's time?"

"Of course, I'll get the bread done." He kissed her again and it occurred to her that she didn't even know his name.

"Thank you, I won't be long."

She grabbed her towel from the hook on the door, and her phone from her bag, and while she waited for the water to heat up, she quickly scrolled through her messages until she found some rather naughty text messages from someone labelled Peter. How had she missed those when she was searching for her mum's number the night before?

She blushed as she scanned their messages back and forth, and wondered what would happen after dinner. She hadn't been with a guy in a very long time. She'd just been too busy to date, and the idea of a full on relationship just hadn't appealed to her. Not to mention her terrible dating past putting her off from trying. But with nothing else to do with her time, it made perfect sense that she would be in a relationship with a serious hunk of a man.

She just hoped she could remember what to do later.

Caru opened Facebook and saw that she had no relationship status listed. Maybe it wasn't serious? She scrolled through her photo albums, and finally found a photo of herself with Peter, on a beach in Bali. She zoomed in on their faces and studied the happy grins. They had travelled together, so surely it must be more than just a fling? She would have to find out without letting on that she had no idea who he was. She searched Facebook for his profile but found none. He didn't seem to be on Instagram either. His apparent lack of social media would definitely make things more difficult.

Caru showered, then got dressed in the only non-black items in her wardrobe – some soft, well-worn light blue jeans and a pale pink jumper.

She was greeted with a refilled glass of wine and another sweet kiss, then led to the table to be seated. She took in all the little details of the table layout and smiled. There was even a single red rose in a vase. She'd never been wined and dined before. But she felt she could easily get used to it.

"Thank you, Peter," she said, trying his name out and hoping she'd got it right.

"I knew it! You *are* annoyed with me. You only ever call me Peter when you're pissed off," he said, bringing her plate over, and setting it down in front of her.

She laughed a bit nervously, glad that she at least had got the right name. "Sorry, baby." Baby? Really? "It's been a weird few days, but I promise I'm not mad with you."

He sat opposite her and placed the garlic bread on the table between them. He reached out to take her hand.

"Promise?"

"Promise," she replied, her tummy flipping from his touch. Or was it from hunger? It was hard to tell. She picked up her fork to dig in. She was so hungry.

"Good." Peter pulled back and picked up his own fork.

"So tell me about your trip," she said, hoping to glean some information from him without him realising what she was doing. Luckily, he was more than happy to share and Caru listened intently while eating the most delicious lasagne she'd ever had.

In short, it seemed he was an archaeologist, and he had been on a dig in South America, which, he very handily reminded her, was where they'd met. It was no wonder they'd never met in her old life. She'd never been to South America before.

She wished that she could remember all the details.

"Tell me about the day we met," she said, finishing the last of her meal and sipping more wine. She rarely drank, and she was glad she now had a full stomach, because she could feel the alcohol beginning to go to her head.

Peter frowned. "What do you mean? You were there."

She shrugged, trying to be nonchalant. "I know I was there, I just want to hear it from your point of view."

He smiled. "Okay, well, it was three years ago, I had just finished a dig, and was celebrating by visiting Machu Picchu with the team." He sipped some wine, and then sat back in his chair, as though he was seeing the scene in his mind. "We'd only been there an hour or so, and we had climbed up the steps to the top, and I saw this woman, you," he said, looked at her with a grin, "with a great big camera, snapping away and quite honestly, ruining the peace with your incessant clicking."

Caru chuckled. She had noticed the camera bag in her room, but hadn't had a chance to have a look at it. But if her laptop and tablet and car were anything to go by, it would be an expensive one.

"It all happened so quickly, but you were so busy looking through your lens that you didn't realise when you stepped back that you were about to step off the edge of the wall, but luckily I did notice because I grabbed you and saved you from falling and breaking your neck."

Caru tried not to look shocked but wasn't sure she was managing it. "You were my hero," she joked, trying to cover her surprise.

"And that's why you insisted on taking me out for a drink and then we ended up talking all night, and by sunrise, I was a goner. You'd stolen my heart."

Caru could feel tears filling her eyes, and she was surprised at the sudden swelling of emotion. It was the Hollywood 'meet cute' she'd always dreamed of. Travelling in South America, being saved by a beautiful, accomplished man, who could cook, no less. And three years ago? Maybe it was a serious relationship, despite the lack of status on Facebook.

She was certain now, that this had to be the dream. There was no way that life could be this good. She would wake up any moment now, she was sure of it.

"What are you thinking?" Peter asked, interrupting her musings.

Caru smiled at him and dabbed her mouth with her napkin (real fabric, he'd thought of everything). "You just tell it so well, it's a beautiful story."

"I'm not a writer, but it will be a good one to tell the kids one day."

Caru nearly choked on her wine again. "Kids?" She coughed. Definitely serious.

"Of course, we have enough saved to get a house now, and my boss promised that I could stick to UK digs after this year. I was thinking actually, that we should have another look around, see what's available. It's a buyer's market right now."

Caru was aware that her eyes were wide and her mouth was slightly agape, but there was nothing she could do about it. She just nodded and let him continue to chatter away about their future together while she finished eating the best piece of garlic bread she'd ever tasted.

CHAPTER NINE

THE following Saturday, Caru took the day off from the agency, leaving a very excited Becky in charge, and she was getting ready to be picked up by Peter. They were going house hunting.

As she searched through her wardrobe for something to wear, she thought back over the previous week. Their first night together had been incredible. He was as good in bed as he was a cook. And boy, did he have some stamina. Caru felt like she needed to start working out in order to keep up. It had taken a couple of days, but Caru soon got used to the naughty text messages he sent frequently, and now enjoyed the blush across her cheeks as she read them in her breaks at work. Becky had commented on her glow, and she couldn't help but giggle out loud as she flicked through her clothes. Only Jess knew why she was glowing so much this week.

She really was a different person. Caru hadn't really

considered that she might be missing out by staying single, and she still knew that she would rather be single than be with the wrong guy. But the feeling of being safe in his embrace was hard to erase from her mind now, and she wondered why she had insisted on trying to do everything by herself for so long. Her mind flitted to her father, and she sighed. Perhaps without believing that he had loved her, she had never opened herself up to the possibility of a loving relationship. A man who actually cared about her feelings, her needs. Her desires. She blushed again.

Caru held up yet another black dress to her body and looked in the mirror with a sigh. It was interesting that this life was so vibrant, yet her wardrobe was so dull. It did make getting dressed easier when everything matched, but she didn't really feel it was doing much for her appearance. She put the dress back and pulled out another, deciding that it looked smart, even if it was boring. She dug through a box of scarves and once she had the little black dress on, she added an orange scarf to try and lift it a little. She wanted to look professional so that the estate agents would take her seriously.

Once she was happy with her appearance, she slipped on her flat back shoes and picked up her handbag. She glanced around the room, amazed that it still looked pristine despite her trying on half her wardrobe. Somehow it felt natural to tidy up as she went along and not leave a trail of destruction. She wondered where that new habit had originated.

"Have fun!" Jess said, popping her head around the door. She looked Caru up and down and whistled. "Nice. So has he popped the question yet or what?"

Caru laughed. "Don't be silly," she said. "We're just

looking at houses." She went to the bathroom to apply some mascara and lip gloss, and Jess followed her, a bemused look on her face.

"Uh huh, you're looking at buying a house together, but getting married? Oh, that would be silly!" Jess raised an eyebrow. "Just promise me you will say yes, and if you find the perfect place, you will go for it. I will find another crazy housemate, please don't worry about me."

"Thank you," Caru said, although if she was honest, she'd been so caught up in the romance of having her own home, she hadn't even considered the fact that she would be leaving Jess without a housemate.

"I'm off shopping with Kate. I'll see you later?"

"Yeah, see you later," Caru replied, as Jess left the room and headed out of the flat. She heard the front door close and she turned to the mirror and looked into her own eyes.

Who was she? Was she really the kind of person who put herself first? Who didn't consider the feelings and needs of others above her own?

It wasn't who she used to be, but then, how many opportunities had she missed, trying to make everyone else happy?

All the opportunities that she now had, it seemed.

"I know it has all the features we want, but it doesn't quite feel..." Peter's voice trailed off as he looked around the empty room that would become the living room.

"Like home?" Caru asked, following his gaze.

Peter looked at her, his face lighting up as if she had said something particularly wise.

"Exactly. It feels cold, uninviting."

Caru shivered at his words. That was exactly how it felt. Like someone else's home, not theirs.

"But with the right furniture and some redecoration, and your own personal things, it could be beautiful," the estate agent said, trying to put a positive spin on things.

It was the fourth house they'd looked at, and Caru felt that he was beginning to get bored. His tone of voice had certainly lost the eagerness to please.

"We're not in a rush," Caru said touching Peter's arm. "We can wait for the right one. At least we know what we don't want."

She saw the estate agent's eyes roll and she ignored him and took the hand Peter offered. They left the house and headed for the car. It seemed pointless to linger any longer than necessary.

"Do you want to see the last one on the list?" Peter asked, holding out the details for her to see when they got back to the car.

Caru scanned the paper, but didn't feel very excited about what she read. It seemed a bit small, and a bit further away from town than they had planned to be. She shrugged. "I guess we might as well? We could go to the Mexican place in town after, on our way back to mine? I'm so hungry."

Peter took the papers back and nodded. "Perfect idea." He leaned down to kiss her, then called out to the agent. "See you at the next one."

The estate agent gave a grimly resigned nod and got in his own car. Peter and Caru looked at one another and both started to giggle. Though it felt like she'd barely known him more than a few days, they seemed to understand each other so easily, they had a connection that transcended normal communication. She had never experienced that with anyone before, and she quite liked it.

There were no words to adequately describe the rush that filled Caru's body when she stepped out of Peter's car and looked up at the house that she knew, without a shred of a doubt, would be their new home.

She looked across the car roof to see Peter staring at the building. He looked the way she felt. And when he turned to her, she knew without even asking that he was thinking exactly what she was thinking.

Caru didn't even stop for a moment to question how she knew, she just closed the car door, and joined Peter and the estate agent at the front door of her new home. The rush of calm euphoria continued to flood through her body.

The front garden was overgrown, and the paint was peeling from the front door, and it was clear that the house had not been cared for in recent years. But the moment they stepped over the threshold and Caru followed the two men into the living room, she felt tears begin to fill her eyes.

It was perfect.

The estate agent clearly was not a good reader of body language, and their reverent silence and the tears in her eyes were misread completely.

"We have more houses coming onto the market all the time," he said with a sigh, not even attempting to sell them the house's features. "I'll make some notes and get back to you next week." He didn't sound hopeful. Clearly, he had written them off.

He was heading back to the front door when Caru finally found her voice.

"We'll take it."

The estate agent stopped in his tracks with a comical skid and his head whipped around. "What?"

Caru looked at Peter for confirmation, and he took her hand and nodded. "We'll take it," Peter said. "It's exactly right."

"Oh! Um, right, um, well do you want to see the rest of it?"

Caru didn't need to, but she and Peter viewed the rest of the property. Her heart swelled at the sight of the high ceilings, the original Victorian features, and the beautiful, if completely overgrown, back garden.

"So are you still interested?" the estate agent asked, suddenly looking very enthusiastic and eager again.

"We'd like to put in an offer. Obviously, it is going to need a lot of work. What do you think the owners would be willing to accept?"

Caru wandered away from the men as they began to discuss figures, and went to explore the garden. She knew she should participate in the negotiations but she didn't care how much it cost. She just knew this would be her new home.

It was difficult to get too far into the garden because of the brambles, but she could see the potential. Even if she didn't have particularly green fingers.

She closed her eyes and imagined the garden all neatly tended to, filled with flowers, and maybe even some raised beds with vegetables growing. In her mind she saw a small dog running around, chased by a small dark haired child who was giggling.

She opened her eyes and stared at the brambles. Was she really imagining her own child? She still couldn't quite believe that she was about to purchase her first home. With her serious boyfriend. A dog seemed feasible, but children too? That was a step beyond anything she could have imagined just a few weeks ago.

Was it real? Or was it just some strange dream she would wake up from eventually? It felt like it had gone on too long for it to simply be a dream. But what about the life in which she had a million hobbies, and worked in an art gallery, and bought a cup of tea for a perfect stranger every day?

That life had been such a struggle. Despite her love of being creative, surviving on the bare minimum of cash was stressful. Running her own business (especially when she couldn't remember so much) had its own stresses, but the Time Traveller Agency was doing well, and she had even been considering hiring another staff member so they could book more tours.

She closed her eyes again and tilted her head toward the sun that was weakly attempting to break through the late afternoon clouds. She had a fleeting thought that she wished her mum could had been there to see her. She would have been so proud of all Caru had accomplished. She decided to take some flowers to her grave the next day, and fill her in on all the latest developments. Her mum was the only one she could talk freely to about this weird reality switch. And even though she didn't get any reply, it made her feel better to talk about it.

Caru opened her eyes and stared up at the house. She saw Peter wave from the window and she smiled.

She hoped that this wasn't all just a vivid dream, because if it was, she didn't want to wake up.

CHAPTER TEN

CARU finished the final sentence of her latest travel article, which she had written about a local castle that she and Peter had visited the day after their house hunt on the weekend. After a quick proofread, she sent it off to the editor of the travel magazine she apparently wrote for. Despite having at least a dozen editions of the magazine bearing her by-line already, she felt a rush of excitement at being published in such a well-known publication. She had only managed to get into local magazines in her other life. As a child she had dreamed of being a travel writer, of visiting hidden places, discovering different cultures and capturing them with her words for others to read. But she had lacked the drive to make it happen. Getting published was hard, and there were so many rules. She had started working in an office straight out of school and began her minimum wage rut.

Her happy feeling now completely deflated, she set

her Mac aside on the bed with a sigh. Then she got up and without thinking about it, neatly folded her clothes that she'd worn to work, put away her shoes and hung up her jacket. She glanced around her room, satisfied that everything was in its place.

She picked up her empty mug and went to the kitchen. She needed to start making some dinner, but was lacking inspiration. Unfortunately, it seemed that she didn't have any magical cooking skills in this life.

"Hey, do you want to go totally against our usual stance on takeaways and get something delivered? I'm just so tired tonight," Jess asked when she entered the kitchen. Caru grinned at her housemate who was washing up at the sink and flicked the kettle on.

"Yes. Absolutely, emphatically yes. You basically just read my mind," Caru said, tipping out the dregs from her cup into the sink and grabbing a new tea bag.

"I just can't bear the idea of cooking," Jess said, hopping onto a kitchen stool and scrolling through menus on her phone. "I figured we both deserve a treat."

It still amazed Caru that they hardly ever bought takeaways. But then, with Peter cooking fabulous meals, and Jess suddenly being a great cook, and her not spending frivolously, it made sense.

"We absolutely deserve a treat," Caru said, pouring some tea.

"What do you fancy? Mexican?"

"Nah, me and Peter had Mexican on the weekend after we found our house," Caru said nonchalantly.

Jess slammed her phone down. "You found a house? Seriously? Tell me everything."

Caru dunked the bag a few more times before

removing it and adding some coconut milk. She turned to her friend and grinned. "It's perfect."

"Has he popped the question yet? You're not getting any younger you know. You need to get married and start having kids." Jess' expression was wide-eyed and innocent, and her tone was teasing despite her cutting words.

Caru held up her hand. "Whoa now. I don't even know if I want to have kids. What's the rush?" She pushed away the vision she'd had of the dark-haired child and frowned. "I'm not THAT old."

Jess giggled. "Sorry, it's just because you're older than me, and even I feel too old already. Besides, I thought you did want to have kids."

"Cheers," Caru said sarcastically. She sighed. "I don't know, maybe I should talk to Laura."

Jess picked up her phone to look at menus again. "Laura?"

"Yeah, she has three kids and a husband, she'd be able to give me some advice."

"Is she someone from work?"

Caru frowned. "No, she's my best friend from school. I go to visit her sometimes?"

Jess shook her head. "Never heard you mention her before."

Caru opened her mouth to insist that she had, but then closed it again. Were she and Laura not friends in this reality? Now that she thought about it, she hadn't heard from her once since she had shifted realities. And it wasn't like her friend to refrain from nagging her to visit her and the children.

"Oh, um maybe I haven't," she said vaguely, picking up her phone and scrolling through her contacts.

Laura's number wasn't there.

"Indian?" Jess asked, waving her phone.

"Um, sure," Caru said, feeling relieved that of the only five numbers she had ever memorised, Laura's was one of them. "Why don't you order for us both? You know what I like. Just tell me how much I owe you. I need to call, um, Peter."

Jess rolled her eyes. "Okay, okay, no need to rub your blissfully beautiful relationship in my face."

Caru tried to smile but was sure it was more of a grimace. She backed out of the kitchen, her mug of tea grasped tightly in one hand, her phone in the other.

Once back in her immaculate room, she set the tea down on the desk, feeling so flustered she forgot to use a coaster. She tapped Laura's number into her phone, and then gulping in a breath, hit the green button.

It rang several times, but eventually, her friend's familiar voice filtered through. Her heart seized up in relief and joy, but then stuttered in panic because she had no idea what to say.

"Hello?" Laura repeated a second time.

"Um, hi," Caru choked out. "It's me, Caru."

"Caru? Caru Jones? Oh my god, really? It's been so long! How are you?"

Caru struggled to swallow. "I'm good," she replied, realising that her voice sounded strangled and not good at all. "How are you?"

"Well, I'm good too, I suppose," Laura said with her usual self-deprecating chuckle. "Still a mess though."

"A mess?"

Laura was the one who had it all figured out. Caru glanced around her Instagrammable bedroom. She was the one who was usually the mess.

"Yeah well, still single, still trying to find the perfect man, still temping! Can't even get a permanent job, let alone a permanent man."

Caru's eyes were wide as she thought of Laura's husband and three beautiful, if loud and often dirty, children.

"Um, so you don't have kids?" Caru asked, her voice dropping to nearly a whisper.

Laura laughed. "Kids? Goodness, no. I can barely make enough money to look after myself."

Caru closed her eyes and felt tears forming. She cast her mind back ten years in her other life.

She remembered how Laura and Rob had met. It was Caru who had accidentally introduced them to each other at her birthday party. She had invited some friends from her work (when she worked in an office) and he had come with them.

But in this reality, she had likely never worked at that office. Or any other minimum wage job. And she and Laura weren't friends in this reality. Which meant Laura and Rob had never met. They hadn't fallen madly in love, married five months later, and gone on to produce three children.

Tears began rolling down her face.

"How long has it been?" she managed to ask.

"Since I last had sex? Or since we last spoke?" Laura asked with a chuckle.

Caru laughed too and wiped her face with her sleeve. "Since we last spoke."

"Um, maybe it was that terrible party we had in sixth form? You know, the one where Maisy threw up all over everyone sitting on the sofa? I think it was just after we'd finished our A-Level exams."

"Really?" Caru asked. "That was the last time?" She cast her mind back. In her reality, she hadn't stayed on at sixth form. She had left school at 16 to start working. But from the sound of it, she had stayed in education longer in this life. But she still hadn't stayed in touch with her oldest friend.

"Yeah I think so. You headed off to Thailand, and Hong Kong, and Australia, and goodness knows where else. And I went to University. I think you had the better idea! My degree in French and German has been completely useless to me. And I can still barely speak a word of either. I started temping after I graduated and have gone from job to job ever since." Laura chuckled again.

"And we just lost touch," Caru said, trying to keep her voice from wavering too much. How was it possible? How could they have drifted so far apart? Why hadn't they emailed? She held back more tears, but it was difficult knowing that Laura's beautiful children didn't exist in this reality.

"Yeah we both got busy. I read all your articles though. Have you written any more recently?"

Caru was surprised that Laura had still followed her career, despite their lack of communication.

"I've just submitted one," she said. "It should be in the next issue."

"Oh that's great, I'll look out for it."

There was a long silence. This never normally happened in their conversations, they always had so much to talk about, no matter how long they went without talking. Caru felt a bit sad that she had delayed visiting Laura because she was too worried about finishing the baby blanket. She realised now that her friend would have wanted to see her with or without a present for the baby.

"Are you happy?" she asked Laura finally, unable to bear another moment of unnatural quiet. She heard her friend sigh loudly.

"I don't know. Are you?"

"I am, but, well, not all the time," Caru said, not really knowing what to say. How could she tell Laura about her amazing boyfriend, her flourishing business and buying her first house, when Laura was still single, still temping, and obviously not enjoying it?

"I guess that's something," Laura said. "Well, it's been good chatting. Call again sometime so we can catch up properly. Maybe we could even meet up for a drink."

"I'd like that," Caru said, her voice cracking. "I'll call you."

"Bye then!"

"Bye." Caru pressed the red button and stared down at her phone with a heavy heart. The gut wrenching agony of Laura's family being stripped away had brought back the fear she had felt when she'd first found herself in this strange new reality. It wasn't fair that she finally got to have everything she wanted, only for everyone else to lose so much. Even if they had no idea what they'd lost.

"It'll be here in ten minutes!" Jess yelled from the kitchen.

"Coming!" Caru yelled back. She rubbed her eyes and sighed. Was having her own business, a boyfriend and buying a house worth the cost of losing her very best friend?

She tapped a quick text to Peter to say she loved him and missed him, then put her phone on her bed and picked up her cup. She sipped some of the cooling tea and winced. She was certain she was going to need something a little stronger.

"Are you okay?"

Caru looked up at Peter from her full dinner plate and blinked. "What?"

He repeated his question, and Caru nodded, putting the forkful of food she'd been moving around her plate into her mouth. It was cold. Even Peter's amazing cooking wasn't improving her mood. She'd barely been able to eat more than a few mouthfuls.

"Why don't I believe you?"

Caru swallowed the food and sighed. Despite feeling like she'd only met him a few weeks before, he really could read her like a book. "It's just a thing with a friend. I thought we were close, but I realised a couple of days ago that I was wrong. It's just bothering me, that's all."

"Did she let you down? What happened?"

Caru felt tears starting to prick her eyelids and she swigged a mouthful of wine. No, she wanted to say. She was the one who had let her friend down. "I'm not sure I'm ready to talk about it," she said, wishing for once that Peter was less caring and kind.

He reached across the dining table and put his hand over hers. "Okay, but I'm here when you're ready."

Caru smiled, grateful that he was going to drop the subject. "Thank you. I'll try to shake off the mood. Dinner was lovely." She put her fork down, and winced, hearing the insincerity in her own voice.

She was pleased when they'd settled on the sofa in front of the TV, so she could let her mind wander without causing suspicion.

In the few days since her conversation with Laura, she hadn't been able to concentrate on anything. All she could think of were Laura's three beautiful children. Harriet, Joy and little Mary. None of whom existed in this world she found herself in. A lump rose in her throat and her eyes filled. She said a silent thanks for the movie they were watching having a poignant moment that could explain her tears if needed.

How could she live in a world where they didn't exist?

And then there was Charlie.

The tears began to flow freely now, and she was aware that she hadn't allowed herself to really grieve for him. It felt silly, as she hadn't even known his name until she had learned of his death. But she was grieving. She was grieving the loss of his soulful voice on the breeze floating up the cobblestones to the gallery. She was grieving his beautiful smile as he reached out for the cup of tea offered to him, his fingers pink from cold, despite his tatty blue fingerless gloves. She was grieving his clear grey eyes, closed when singing, bright and sparkling when talking to her about the weather.

She was trying to hold in the sobs, but her shuddering shoulders alerted Peter that there was something amiss. He paused the movie and pulled her in tighter.

"Hey," he said. "What is it? You don't normally get this upset over films."

Caru cried for several minutes before she was able to calm down enough to speak, and when she did, she couldn't stop herself from blurting out. "They're all dead, because of me, and I don't know if I can ever make it right."

"What on earth do you mean? Who's dead?"

Caru shook her head and let the sobs take over. She had no idea how she could possibly explain any of it to Peter, when she didn't even understand it herself.

Peter allowed her to cry for a while, then he wrapped a blanket from the back of the sofa around her shaking shoulders, and got up to get her a glass of whisky.

It was Jess's whisky, but Caru didn't protest. She figured her housemate wouldn't mind too much.

A while later, when she was much calmer, Peter tried again.

"Who is dead? Why is it your fault? I don't understand."

Caru sniffled. "I don't know how to explain, but there are people who should exist, beautiful people, and they don't. All because of me."

Peter frowned. "I still don't understand. They died? Or never existed?"

Caru stared into Peter's eyes, which looked so dark in the dim light of the TV screen, but she knew in reality were a pale hazel. "Both."

Peter raised an eyebrow, but said nothing.

"I can't explain right now, but I promise, when I figure out how to, I will. I haven't actually killed anyone. It's just impossible to explain. I'm sorry about the crying, I thought I had everything under control, but it just hit me all at once then, and I didn't know what to do."

Peter pulled her into his arms again. "Never apologise for feeling emotional. To be honest, although I admit to being quite confused by what you've said, I'm kind of glad as you've never really expressed much emotion over things before, and I was worried you were holding everything in too much. It's good to let it out every now and then."

Caru was surprised. In her former life she was very emotional, prone to crying over adverts. Had feeling as though her dad had loved her, been enough to turn her into a more resilient and less emotional person? She decided to go back to the cemetery to visit her mother's grave again. Maybe talking through everything out loud would help her to process. Her mum had always loved Laura when they were teenagers. She would understand the loss that Caru felt over their friendship.

"I'm feeling much better," she said, pulling back a little to kiss Peter softly. "Thank you. Shall we watch the rest of the movie?"

"Were you really watching it? Because actually, I think I need to head home, got an early start."

"You're not staying?" Caru hated the needy tone in her voice, but she felt like she needed some extra support right then.

"I wasn't going to, but I can. I will just have to leave even earlier."

"I don't mind an early start," Caru said, trying not to sound too eager.

Peter smiled and smoothed her cheek with his thumb. "Okay, let's go to bed then."

Caru nodded and got up, folding the blanket and placing it on the back of the sofa. She quickly cleared up, putting their dishes in the dishwasher and turning off the TV. Less than fifteen minutes later, they were in her bed, and Peter was doing his very best to take her mind off of other realities.

CHAPTER ELEVEN

"WITH the way everything is going forward, we will be moving in by the 20th."

Caru's heart felt heavy as Jess's face fell, she felt bad for leaving her housemate just before Christmas. They'd always had such a great time together over the winter. But she was eager to get into her new place. It was going to take quite a bit of work, but they'd decided to move straight in, and slowly do it up, room by room, exactly how they wanted.

"We can still go ice-skating," Caru said.

"Really? I thought you hated ice-skating?"

Caru frowned. Memories of previous Christmases, the two of them laughing and chasing each other around the rink filled her head. "Oh, well, I know you enjoy it, so we should do it."

Jess tried to smile. "Cool." She started emptying the dishwasher, and the sound of the dishes clanging together made Caru wince. "I guess I should start advertising your room then, if that's okay?"

Caru nodded, but she was close to tears. She wondered briefly if she was hormonal, it seemed like all she wanted to do was cry recently. "Good idea. I'll keep it as tidy as possible so people can see it."

Jess forced a chuckle. "It's always tidy. I've never seen a thing out of place in there."

The state of her room in her former existence flashed through Caru's mind like a distant hazy memory and she smiled. If only this Jess knew! She wished she could tell her housemate everything. She felt terrible for keeping such a huge secret from everyone, but who would even believe her? At least she could talk to her mum. It helped, even if she never got a reply.

She hugged her housemate, then went to get ready for work. It had been nearly two months since she had shifted to this reality, and aside from her emotional outburst to Peter a week prior, she had settled into her new routine quite easily and effortlessly, as though it really was her life. Her heart still ached at the thought of Laura's children and of Charlie, but as long as she kept busy, she could keep the tears from bubbling up. With each day that passed, it felt like her old life was merely a dream, and that it hadn't really happened. She wasn't a messy, creative hoarder who spent all her money on craft supplies, who had never really grown up, who lacked love, security and real connection.

She was a sensible, clean, tidy, financially savvy adult who was in the process of buying her first house with her very serious and seriously gorgeous boyfriend. She was a woman who was confident in her own abilities, and laser focused on her career as a travel writer and travel agent.

Caru was just picking up her keys from her desk and her scarf and coat from the hook on the back of her door, when it struck her.

Despite having it all, she still wasn't happy. But why? She had everything she had ever dreamed of as a child. She lacked nothing. She paused at the door and surveyed her room, and the stark decor made her shiver.

It was devoid of warmth, of life, of colour. All the things that she associated with joy. She glanced at the empty corner of the room where her print table had once been, and she closed her eyes briefly and remembered the feeling of the sticky ink, the rollers going over the type, and the impression on the paper being created with a satisfying clunk of the Adana handle being pressed down.

She missed it. She missed the creativity, the mess, the joy of creating simple things.

Caru opened her eyes and sighed. She didn't miss the stress and struggle of not having enough money though. But perhaps the reason she wasn't happy was because she had brought her old emotions and beliefs with her. And she still felt that hollow feeling of lack, deep at her core, that apparently hadn't existed in this life.

Shaking her head at her own whirling thoughts and emotions, Caru headed for the door of the flat, shrugging on her thick winter coat and wrapping her scarf around her neck. She locked the flat behind her, and headed downstairs and outside to her car, shivering in the bitter wind that whipped around her face. By the time she reached her pink Mini, she was berating herself for not picking up her hat and gloves too. It was a bitterly cold November so far, and apparently they might even see snow by the weekend.

She got into the car and started the engine, pressed the seat warmer button, and rubbed her hands together.

She glanced at her phone and smiled at the message Peter had sent. Her mind shifted to thinking about how they would decorate their new home together, and she shoved her uneasiness to the back of her mind, where it couldn't ruin her day.

"The usual?"

Caru nodded at the barista, then paid with her card, got her loyalty card stamped, and moved to the other end of the counter to wait for her order. She had started going back to the coffee shop in the morning, mainly because the coffee machine at work had broken, and partly because it made her feel more normal, more like her old self.

She picked up her coffee and smiled at the barista, noting with a smile that her name was spelled correctly on the cup, written in neat script with a little heart next to it.

A small part of her wished they would spell it wrong, just once, just so it would feel right. She headed outside, and hurried past Charlie's doorstep to her travel agency down the side street.

The run up to Christmas was a busy time for them, with people booking to go away over the holiday to see the northern lights, Santa in Lapland, or at the complete opposite end of the scale, to the hottest places possible to escape the cold. She wished she was going away too, but with the sale of the house now going through, her savings were quite empty, and she and Peter had decided to wait until the following spring or even summer before they went on holiday together. She didn't have any travel booked for writing articles about, but she had been going through some travel brochures and dreaming of the places she would like to see. She was hoping she could fit in at least a couple of trips in the next year, she couldn't just write about places in the UK for the magazine, they would need more exciting material.

She reached the agency and unlocked the door. She tapped in the code on the door, and then switched on the lights, and the heaters, and booted up her computer. She set her paper cup on her desk and then took off her coat and hung it up before settling down in her chair.

Becky was off for a week, and Caru had managed to get her to remind her of the alarm code before she left. Otherwise she would have been a bit stuck.

She got so lost in the rhythm of emails and queries and updating the website deals and collating information for their spring catalogue, that it was past lunchtime before she noticed the time. The bell at the door rang and she looked up to see Pat from the bakery standing there holding her usual lunch order.

"Hungry?" Pat asked with a grin.

Caru laughed and grabbed her purse. She went over to Pat, handed her the money and took the bag. "Starving," she said. "Got carried away. Thank you. You didn't have to drop it in, I would have come over eventually."

Pat waved her hand and smiled. "No problem, can't have my regulars passing out with hunger."

Caru smiled. "Thank you."

Pat left and headed back up the street to her bakery,

and Caru sat back at her desk and tucked into her cheese and onion baguette.

But for some reason, after only a few mouthfuls, she felt a bit queasy. She wrapped up the remaining baguette, but even the smell of it next to her was making her nauseated. She got up to take the baguette remains to the small kitchenette, but when she got there she began to heave, and only managed to get to the sink before throwing up.

Feeling drained and bewildered, she wiped her mouth with some kitchen towel and drank some water to try and rinse the taste of sick from her mouth.

She'd never had a problem with cheese and onion before. It wasn't like it could be off, it wasn't meat.

Her stomach growled and churned, and she rested a hand there, wondering what had upset it.

A memory flashed through her mind of her friend Laura cradling her belly in the same way when she was expecting Harriet.

Caru's eyes widened, and she staggered over to her desk to get her diary out of her bag. She flipped to September and October, and sure enough, she hadn't had a period since the middle of September. Which meant she was three weeks late. How had she not noticed? How had this happened? She and Peter had been careful. Surely she couldn't be pregnant?

She sat heavily in her chair, her heart racing at the idea. Peter had mentioned children during dinner that first time, and seemed to think it would naturally follow once they moved in together, but aside from her vision in the garden, Caru hadn't really thought about having children. She'd never really felt particularly maternal, despite loving her friends' children. But was that because her own father had abandoned her? Would this version of herself have been more excited about the idea? She had the feeling that maybe she would have. There was certainly a tiny stirring of excitement within her that she never would have thought possible. Despite that, the idea of having a child was still overwhelming. Tears filled her eyes and she sighed. At least it explained her recent overly emotional state.

Before she could get too overwhelmed, or indeed, too excited, Caru decided to go and buy a test. There was no point getting all wound up for no reason.

She slipped her coat and scarf on, and headed for the door, flipping the closed sign before locking it behind her. She headed to the high street, going straight to the pharmacy. She didn't even bother trying to hide her purchase, she just picked up two boxes of tests and went straight to the counter.

The cashier smiled at her while she served her and scanned the boxes, but Caru couldn't bring herself to smile back. She just took her receipt and tucked the boxes inside her coat, muttering a thank you before making a swift exit.

She walked quickly back to the agency, and left the closed sign showing while locking the door behind her.

She knew the tests were best done first thing in the morning, but she couldn't wait. She pulled off her coat and headed straight to the toilet which was in a tiny cupboard space.

Five minutes later, she was sat at her desk, staring at the two pink lines in a state of shock.

She was pregnant. With Peter's child. They were having

a baby. Despite the fear and amazement and shock in her system, she couldn't help thinking of the smaller spare room in their new home, which would make the perfect nursery.

Tears filled her eyes and spilled over. She wished she could call Laura to tell her the amazing news, but they weren't really friends anymore. She knew Jess would be pleased for her, but it wouldn't be quite the same as telling her very best friend.

Knowing that she wouldn't be able to concentrate on work for the rest of the day, and still feeling a bit queasy, Caru decided to close early and head home, so she could get used to this new idea, and figure out how she would tell Peter when he came over for dinner that evening.

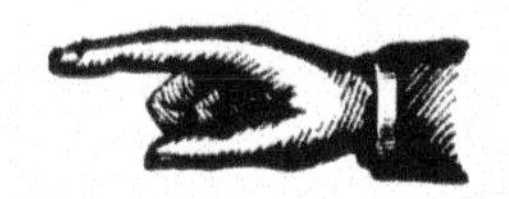

CHAPTER TWELVE

CARU was nervously stirring the white sauce, hoping that the smell of lasagne wouldn't make her throw up, when Peter arrived. She was following a recipe he had written out for her, but hadn't used onions in the tomato sauce, just in case they had been the reason she'd been ill earlier that day.

She buzzed him into the building, and then went straight back to the sauce, quickly whisking out the lumps that managed to form in the twenty seconds she'd left it alone.

When she felt Peter's arms circle her waist and his scent filled the air around her, she closed her eyes briefly and sighed. He really did make her feel calm, and safe.

"How was your day?" he murmured into her hair.

Caru opened her eyes and continued stirring, unsure whether to just blurt it out, or to present the information to him once they had sat down to eat.

"It was busy," she said finally, opting for a later reveal. "Wine?"

Peter took the glass she offered him, but didn't comment on the fact that she was sipping water. She thought back to all the times she'd drunk alcohol over the last five weeks, and wondered how many of those had been drunk while she was pregnant. Her mum had always sworn that she'd still drunk a glass of wine occasionally while pregnant with her, and she'd turned out fine, so what was the harm?

"Are you okay?"

Caru blinked and looked up at Peter. She switched the heat off under the sauce, then started assembling the lasagne in the glass dish, starting with the tomato sauce on the bottom. "Yes, sorry, were you saying something?" She pulled the sheets of uncooked lasagne out of the box and started laying them on top.

Peter smiled, but he looked concerned. "I was saying that my mum was harassing me about seeing us over Christmas. I tried to explain that it would be our first in our new house, but she was insistent. I said I would ask you, but it would be Christmas Eve or Boxing Day, and she told me not to wait too long to let her know."

Caru smiled. "I'd love to meet your mum, but let's invite her over for Boxing Day. Then she can see the house."

Peter set his glass down. "Um, you've already met her? At my sister's wedding last year?" Caru's heart rate quickened and she accidentally slopped white sauce over the side of the dish onto the counter and the floor, narrowly missing her sock.

Caru forced a laugh. "Of course! I meant I'd love to

meet up with her. I remember the wedding." She shook her head. "My mind is not on form today."

Peter picked up a sponge from the sink and wiped the counter, then he took Caru's hands in his and made her look at him.

"What is it? Something's wrong."

It wasn't a question. It was a statement. He really did know her too well. It was quite disconcerting.

"I'm pregnant," she blurted out.

His eyes nearly popped out of his head at her blunt words and his grip tightened on her hands.

"What?" he sputtered.

She just nodded.

A smile spread across his face and he pulled her into his arms in a crushing hug. "That's amazing! Are you sure? How far along?"

Caru laughed in relief that he was happy, and fought to breathe in his grip. "I did a test at work, then another when I got home, and I had some sickness. I don't know how far, but I'm three weeks late, so it could be up to five weeks."

Peter's eyes widened. "The night I got back from the dig? But we were careful."

Caru chuckled. "I know."

Peter kissed her. "Can I see the test?"

Caru smiled. "Sure, it's in my room, I'll go get it." She waved at the half-assembled lasagne. "Can you salvage that?"

Peter chuckled. "Of course."

She went to her bedroom and got the two tests out of her bedside table drawer where she had hidden them. She stared down at them, still unsure how she felt about having a child. It didn't feel real. But that stirring of excitement inside her was growing stronger.

She joined Peter in the kitchen, where he was putting the lasagne in the oven.

Caru handed the tests to him and he stared down at them like they were made of precious materials.

"We're going to be parents?"

His voice was an awed hush, and tears sprang to Caru's eyes.

"Yes," she said, reaching out to wrap her arms around his waist. "We are."

Peter wrapped his arm around her and rested his head against hers. "Good thing we have that spare room in our new home, it will make the perfect nursery."

Caru smiled. "I was thinking the exact same thing."

"Oh my god! Congratulations!"

Caru smiled at Jess who was jumping up and down and squealing.

"Thank you, it's a bit of a shock, to be honest. It's not like we had intended to try. I'm still not used to the idea yet."

"Please tell me he's popped the question now?" Jess poured a glass of whisky for herself, and a glass of water for Caru.

Caru took the water and clinked it against her housemate's glass. "Cheers. And no, he hasn't. But he doesn't have to. Besides, we've spent all our money on buying the house, and we'll need cash for the renovations, and now for nappies! Getting married isn't exactly a priority."

"Maybe not," Jess said, taking a sip of her drink. "But it wouldn't hurt for him to ask!"

Caru chuckled. "I'm in no hurry. I'm still trying to process this new development."

"Have you made an appointment to see the doctor? Do you know how many weeks?"

Caru shook her head. "I literally found out on Friday, so I haven't called the doctors yet. I'll do it tomorrow at work. It would be good to know how many weeks."

"You found out on Friday and you are only telling me now?" Jess demanded.

Caru raised an eyebrow. "You weren't here? How was your date, by the way?"

Jess blushed. "It was good. In fact, he's actually looking for somewhere to rent. I was thinking he could come look at your room."

Caru nearly choked on her water. "After one date you're thinking of living with him? That must have been some date! Tell me more."

Jess grinned and poured some more whisky. "Happy to oblige! Let's make some food and have a good catch up."

"Sounds good to me," Caru agreed. "But no onions, please. They make me want to puke at the moment."

"No onions, got it."

"You really don't want to tell anyone?"

It was a week later, and after seeing the doctor and finding out she was six weeks pregnant, Caru was out for dinner with Peter at their favourite Mexican restaurant.

Which wasn't the best choice because it seemed like everything had onions in it.

"I just think we should wait until twelve weeks before we tell everyone. I've told Jess and Becky, but that's only because I can't hide the morning sickness. Which, by the way, doesn't usually happen in the morning."

Peter put the menu down and sighed. "Okay, so we need to wait until Christmas?"

"Yes, hey, how about we just give everyone a scan photo as a gift? It'll save us a fortune," Caru joked.

Peter chuckled. "My mum would be thrilled with that. She's still pestering my sister about producing grandchildren, but having kids just wouldn't fit into her lifestyle."

Caru nodded, but seeing as she couldn't remember having met his sister, let alone going to her wedding, she also had no idea what she did for a living, or even what her name was... she wondered how she would get that information without it being obvious that she had no memory of his family.

"It's settled then? We'll tell everyone at Christmas?" She had already visited her mum's grave and told her the news, but she figured that didn't really count.

"Okay," Peter agreed. "Now what do you want to order?"

"Plain cheese quesadilla, with sour cream, please. Everything else has onions in it."

Peter winced. "Maybe we should stick to cooking at home, I don't want you feeling queasy."

Caru smiled. "It would save us some money too. We move in just two weeks, we need to cut down on our spending a bit, we still have the moving van to pay for and need to buy some more furniture. Not to mention a fridge and washing machine, and-"

"Okay, okay," Peter said, signalling to the waiter. "We'll stop eating out." He smiled at her and then gave their order to the waiter. The waiter noted their food choices and topped up their water and nachos.

Caru munched on the nachos but ate them dry, even though she knew the salsa was delicious.

"So, what is your sister up to at the moment?" she asked nonchalantly, trying to glean some information without causing suspicion.

Peter sighed. "I spoke to her the other night. She's still flying, even though she's had a cough for weeks. I've told her she needs to take time out, but she and Jim have got used to the money she's on, and she says she can't afford to take the time off. But I think it's ridiculous, flying when you can hardly breathe. Of course, it wouldn't hurt her to stop smoking."

Caru nodded, mentally noting that his sister must be a flight attendant, smoked, and was married to a man called Jim. She kept crunching away on the nachos, and Peter continued.

"Hope has always been a stubborn one. Remember the story I told you about when she broke her toe but refused to stop running the cross country race at school? Her toe was permanently disfigured, all because she wouldn't quit." He took a handful of nachos and dipped a couple in the salsa before popping them in his mouth.

Caru was mentally adding to her notes. His sister's name was Hope. And apparently she was a stubborn woman who wouldn't quit. She would search for his sister on social media, see if she could glean any further information. But not knowing her married name might make it tricky.

"You're very quiet tonight," Peter commented.

Caru sipped some ice water. "Just hungry. And besides, I like hearing about what your family are up to."

Peter smiled and reached across the table to put his hand over hers. "You're amazing. Have I told you that recently?"

Caru chuckled. "No, not recently."

"Well you are." Peter squeezed her hand, and then leaned back to allow the waiter to place the plates on the table in front of them.

The smell of Peter's sizzling burritos made her stomach turn just slightly, but she breathed through her mouth, and waited for the sensation to pass. Luckily, she didn't feel the need to run to the bathroom.

She slowly cut up her quesadilla, and dipped a corner in the sour cream. The plain flavours were soothing, and she practically inhaled it, finishing her meal way ahead of Peter, which was almost unheard of.

He dabbed his mouth with his napkin. "Hungry?" he teased.

"Yep, hurry up, I want dessert."

Peter chuckled and waved the waiter over. "Order now, I'll have my favourite."

Caru smiled and ordered three desserts, knowing that one just wasn't going to be enough for her. She rested her hand on her stomach and wondered how much she would need to eat when the baby began to grow.

"You're eating for three already," Peter teased as she tucked into her desserts when they arrived. "Are you sure it's not twins?" He pretended to try and protect his dessert and she giggled.

"I did warn you it would save us money to eat at home," Caru joked. "And god, I hope not!"

"I think you might be right," Peter wiped his hands on his napkin and started to eat his dessert, but when he looked up and saw Caru's empty plates and longing gaze, he sighed and pushed his own plate closer to her. She grinned at him and helped herself to more than half of his pie.

CHAPTER THIRTEEN

CARU was nearly at the top of the high street, heading for the coffee shop for her morning coffee fix, (though these days she was only on decaf which meant she actually had to get enough sleep) when a sound made her stop in her tracks.

Her heart started thumping in her chest, and she gulped a few deep breaths in, then she closed her eyes, straining to listen.

She heard it again, it was unmistakeable.

It was Charlie.

She opened her eyes but kept her gaze trained on the pavement as she took a few steps forward, afraid to look to see it if really was him. When she was close enough, she looked up and there he was.

His eyes were closed, his fingers were moving deftly on the strings of his battered guitar, his guitar case open in front of him, to gather coins.

Tears began to stream down her cheeks, and Caru moved closer to him, his voice drawing her in.

"Charlie," she whispered as she get closer. "Charlie, you're alive."

He looked up at her then, and their eyes locked. He stopped playing abruptly.

"Caru," he said, pain etched across his face. "I thought you'd left me."

The tears flowed freely now, and the look on his face broke her heart. "I'm so sorry, I had no idea, I mean, I don't even know how. I'm just so, so sorry."

Charlie shook his head. "It's too late. You've made your choice."

Caru frowned and wiped her face with her hand. "What do you mean? I came back, I'm here now."

She blinked and Charlie suddenly vanished. "Charlie?" she said, looking all around her. "Charlie?" She turned in circles searching the street around her but he really had gone. It was too late.

"Charlie!"

"Caru, wake up."

Caru blinked in confusion at Peter, who was peering at her in concern in the dim light of dawn.

"Oh, Peter." She burst into tears and he wrapped his arms around her and pulled her close. She sobbed into his t-shirt, feeling a depth of grief and loss that she hadn't let herself feel before.

After a few moments, her sobs turned into sniffles and she stopped shaking. She felt Peter take a deep breath before he asked quietly.

"Caru, who is Charlie?"

Her breath caught and her mind whirled. "What?" she

whispered into his chest.

Peter pulled away enough to look at her face. "Charlie. You called out his name just now, when you were thrashing about."

Caru let her breath out in a rush. "Oh," she said, wondering how to explain. Did she go for the normal explanation? That he was a busker who died? Or the otherworldly explanation, that he possibly still existed in a parallel universe and was now haunting her dreams?

Peter waited patiently while she gathered her thoughts, but she wondered if he was thinking that she was cheating on him.

"He was a guy I knew, a busker," she started slowly. "He had a beautiful voice." She paused and Peter nodded for her to continue.

"I found out a while ago that he died," she said, her voice reducing to a whisper, a tear falling onto her pillow. "I didn't even find out his name until he was already gone." She bowed her head. "I was just dreaming of him. He was singing on the street, but then he disappeared. It was so real."

Peter looked confused. "Why were you dreaming about a total stranger?"

Caru sighed. "I don't know, I guess because I saw him singing every day, and yet never even knew his name until I found out he'd died."

Peter still looked a bit suspicious, but he leaned forward to kiss her forehead. "I'm sorry. It's hard to lose someone."

Caru shook her head. "I barely knew him, I don't even know why it affected me, or why I am dreaming of him."

Peter smiled. "Sometimes we have a connection to

people that makes no sense. It's okay, maybe you just hadn't processed your grief over his death."

Caru nodded. "I didn't really grieve. I didn't feel like I was allowed to, considering how little I knew of him. And I was distracted by the other things I lost the day I found out that he had died." She stopped, realising that she had said too much.

Peter frowned. "What else did you lose?"

Caru thought of her job at the gallery, of Kevin, of all her many hobbies, of Laura, and her children, and she sighed. "Nothing, it was just a weird day I guess."

She could tell Peter wasn't convinced by her brush off, but she didn't want to go into detail of the other life she had been living. Other than her very vivid dream, more recently her old life had faded and become a distant memory, and she had begun to wonder if maybe it hadn't been real at all. But how could she have imagined it? And if it had been real, why was Charlie haunting her now?

"Would you like some water?" Peter asked, interrupting her internal musings. She nodded and he got up to get her a glass. She lay back and stared up at her ceiling. They were moving to their new home in a week. She would soon be leaving here, and living with Peter all the time.

She lay a hand on her stomach, where she had yet to notice a change. In just seven months they would be welcoming their child into this world. She still couldn't quite believe she was pregnant. Though the daily sickness was hardly imagined. She felt bad for Becky having to put up with her retching at work.

"Here," Peter said, holding a glass out to her.

She sat up and took it from him, sipping the cool liquid. It did make her feel a bit better. She placed the half empty glass on the bedside table as Peter climbed back into bed with her.

She snuggled into his side and closed her eyes against the growing light of the rising sun.

"I'm sorry I woke you. It's silly, really."

"It's not silly at all," Peter said softly. "He obviously had an effect on you."

"He did," she whispered. "He was so talented, it just feels like the world is a bit of a darker place without him in it."

"I'm sure he's in a better place now."

"I hope so," Caru replied, seeing Charlie's anguished expression in her dream. "I really hope so."

"Are you sure you're going to be okay?"

Jess smiled at Caru. "Of course, I'm going to be great. Henry is ready to move in, so I won't be alone for long. Just make sure you come visit!"

Caru's eyes filled with tears. "I'm going to miss you."

"You're only moving to the outskirts of town, not to the moon! We'll see each other all the time, you'll see. Though we might have to give ice-skating a miss, considering your condition and all."

Caru laughed and sniffled, wiping her face with her gloved hand. "Yeah possibly not the best idea. But let's have some dinner. Maybe we could get together over Christmas?"

Jess smiled and hugged Caru. "Sounds perfect. Now get going! You've got a lot of boxes to empty when you get there. Peter is waiting."

Caru nodded and looked down at the keys in her hand. She pulled her keys to the flat off the keyring and handed them to Jess.

"I'll see you soon, roomie."

Jess took the keys and nodded. "Love you."

"Love you," Caru echoed, turning and going down the stairs before she could start sobbing.

She pulled the main door to the building shut behind her, the thunk of the heavy wood hitting the frame making a rather final sound.

She climbed into the front of the van that she and Peter had hired to move their belongings and looked over to him.

"You ok?" he asked, knowing that she wasn't.

She nodded anyway, and he reached across to squeeze her leg.

"You'll see her soon."

Caru tried to smile, but failed. She pulled her seatbelt on as the tears trickled down her face.

"Let's go," she said, her voice wavering.

Peter started the engine and turned around in the driveway, and they set off to their new house, and their new life together.

Caru looked in the side mirror and watched her old home recede into the distance. There was a weird feeling in the pit of her stomach, and she hoped that it was indigestion, and not a sign of something bad.

Twenty minutes later, they pulled into their new driveway, and parked as close to the front door as possible.

Caru got out and breathed in deeply. It was only four o'clock, but darkness was already threatening, and she wasn't sure she had the energy to unload everything before the light faded, but they had to return the van in the morning.

As if he could sense her fatigue, Peter came up behind her and wrapped his arms around her waist.

"Why don't you take the kettle inside, and make us a cuppa and order a takeaway for dinner, while I unload? It shouldn't take me too long."

Caru smiled, feeling genuinely grateful for this amazing human being who seemed so intuitive to her needs.

"That sounds good," she replied. She turned around in his arms and kissed him. "I love you."

Peter kissed her back. "I love you too." He rested a hand on her stomach. "And I love you, little monster."

Caru smiled and kissed him again. "She loves you too."

"She? You think it's a girl?" Peter's face lit up in excitement.

Caru laughed. "I have no idea. But I know the baby is hungry."

Peter chuckled. "We better make sure she gets fed then. Go and order, and get the kettle on."

"On it," Caru said. She accepted the small box he handed her, which contained the kettle, cups, tea and teaspoons, and headed to the door.

"Wait!" Peter called out before she could put the key in the lock.

He came up behind her and scooped her up off her feet. She shrieked and laughed as he opened the door and stepped in, with her in his arms.

"Really?" she sputtered, still laughing. "I didn't realise you were so traditional."

"Of course," Peter said. "Need to do things properly!"

Caru giggled as he kissed her then set her back on her feet. The cups chinked together in the box she was still holding. "You better hope that's not my favourite mug breaking," she warned.

Peter kissed her again. "It'll be fine."

She narrowed her eyes at him. Then she headed to the kitchen, flicking the lights on as she went. The kitchen felt cold, and she shivered. They needed to work out the heating system quickly.

She made two mugs of tea and then got her phone out to order food, and saw a message from Jess saying she hoped they'd got there okay.

Caru smiled and sent a smiley face and a heart back. Then she headed outside to see how Peter was getting on.

CHAPTER FOURTEEN

CARU had hoped that after moving to the new home, she would leave her old reality behind completely, but after waking up on Christmas Eve after yet another dream about Charlie, she was beginning to feel frustrated.

What did it mean? Why was he haunting her? There was nothing she could do for him, he was dead.

Or was he?

The idea that he might be trapped in some in-between world plagued her. Could she help him somehow? Or was he calling her back? To her old life?

Her tummy flipped nervously as she thought about going back. She hated that Charlie was gone, but the idea of losing Peter, her new home, her business, and now her baby, it just didn't bear thinking about.

What was their connection? Why had she felt a bond to the busker? She never did work it out. Maybe her mum would have some ideas. She would ask her later when she visited her.

Caru sighed and looked down at her barely visible bump then smiled, all thoughts of Charlie flying from her mind. They were telling Peter's family on Boxing Day when they came to visit, and she was excited to share their news.

Peter was already up, she could hear him moving in the small spare room next door and she frowned. He had been going in and out of there for a few days now, but had refused to let her in.

She heard the bedroom door open and she got out of bed and turned around to see Peter stood there, a huge grin on his face.

"Merry Christmas, beautiful."

She smiled and pulled her dressing gown on. "Merry Christmas to you too, though you know it's tomorrow, right?"

Peter shrugged. "It might be tomorrow, but I can't wait another day, I need to give you your gift now."

Caru smiled. "Okay, why not?" She closed her eyes and held her hands out, and she heard Peter chuckle. She felt him take her hands and lead her out of the room. They didn't go far before he told her to open her eyes.

She gasped.

The spare room had been transformed into a magical new world. She looked at the murals covering the walls of scenes of their favourite books, and then saw the wooden crib in the corner, and the beautiful restored old rocking chair by the window.

She looked at Peter, her eyes already brimming with tears. "It's amazing," she said. "I can't believe you did this so quickly."

Peter grinned. "I haven't slept much the last few days," he admitted. "But I wanted it to be ready in time to share our news with everyone."

Caru smiled and kissed him, thanking the universe for the millionth time for the amazing man in front of her. "I love it, it's perfect."

Peter sighed dramatically. "Thank goodness. I thought you might make me repaint it magnolia or something."

Caru chuckled. "Hardly, it's amazing." She went closer to the murals to study them more closely, amazed at the detail. "I had no idea you were such a great artist."

Peter laughed. "You know I'm always doodling."

"These are more than doodles," Caru said. "Maybe you should have been an artist instead of an archaeologist."

"Yeah, maybe," Peter said.

Caru ran her hand along the rail of the crib "I was thinking of getting some wool to make a blanket for the baby." Her mind flashed to the blanket she made for Laura's youngest, Mary. The thought gave her an uncomfortable feeling in her stomach but she tried her best to ignore it.

"Sounds good, didn't realise you could knit," Peter commented.

Caru shrugged. "I learned as a kid. I think I can remember how though." The lies rolled easily off her tongue as if they were the truth. Which they were, in this reality.

"Cool. Breakfast?"

Caru's stomach growled in response and she laughed. "Yes, please. I'm starving."

"You're always hungry," Peter teased her as they went

downstairs into the kitchen.

"I can't help it. I am feeding two bellies you know."

"Are you sure it's not three?" Peter laughed.

Caru's heart skipped a beat at the thought of having twins. She was supposed to have had her first scan a few days before, but it had been postponed until the day after Boxing Day. What if there *were* two babies in there?

Peter saw her expression and smiled at her. "I'm just kidding. I'm sure it's not."

"I hope not," Caru said. "Having one seems overwhelming enough, but two?"

"We could do it," Peter said confidently. "I'd just need to get another crib."

"Not to mention a second everything," Caru said, putting the kettle on while Peter set out cereal on the table and put bread in the toaster.

"True, could get more expensive," Peter agreed.

Caru made their drinks and took them to the table and sat down, wrapping her gown around her more tightly and shivering a little. The house seemed to take a little while to warm up in the morning. They planned to put a wood fire in the lounge so it would feel cosier. But it wasn't at the top of their list of priorities.

"So," Peter said, sitting down at the table and pouring too many cornflakes into his bowl. "What shall we do today?"

Caru smiled, even though she knew she would be cleaning up his mess again when he spilled cornflakes all over the floor. "I need to call Jess to wish her a Merry Christmas because it feels like we haven't spoken since I moved out. And then I would love to go for a walk, visit mum, and later watch Christmas movies."

"I'm going to try and finish reading my book. I could come for a walk with you after though."

Caru got up to get the toast. "Sounds good." She knew that it meant she wouldn't be able to chat freely to her mum's grave, but the company would be nice.

They ate breakfast slowly, enjoying a more relaxing start to the day after the previous week of unpacking and sorting and trying to make the house feel like a home. Then Caru cleaned up the dishes and moved into the lounge, sitting on the armchair they'd got second-hand. It was near the radiator so she could stay warm. She picked up the blanket draped over the back of it and wrapped it around her. She would shower and get dressed after talking to her old housemate.

She found Jess's number and hit the green button, then waited for her to pick up.

"Hello?"

Caru frowned. Jess' voice sounded uncertain and fearful.

"Jess, are you okay?" she asked, wondering what was going on.

"Caru, um, yeah, of course," Jess said, but Caru could hear that she was crying.

"Jess, what's wrong?"

There was a pause, and Caru could hear Jess gulping in deep breaths. "Nothing, I'm okay, was just, um, watching a sad movie, and you caught me by surprise."

A sad movie? First thing in the morning on Christmas Eve? It didn't feel like a likely explanation for the sadness in her friend's voice, but Caru could feel Jess pulling away, and she didn't want to push her for an explanation.

"Oh, sorry. I just wanted to wish you and Henry a

Merry Christmas. Are you two ready for tomorrow?"

"Oh, yeah. We're ready, got a roast dinner ready to prepare, and um, yeah the decorations are up."

Caru tried to smile and picture it, but she was having trouble imagining it, considering the quiver in her friend's voice.

They chatted for a few more minutes, but Caru could feel that Jess wasn't really paying much attention to her words.

After hanging up, Caru sat and stared into space for a while before going upstairs to shower. She hoped that her friend would share whatever was upsetting her with her soon. She felt guilty for having moved out, she hated not being there to be a shoulder to cry on.

While she got dressed, Caru sent out a silent prayer for her friend to be protected, then she shook off her fear and worry and resolved to enjoy the rest of the day.

"Merry Christmas!"

Caru opened one eye, feeling a bit bleary after going to bed late after watching a favourite Christmas movie.

She rolled over to see Peter smiling at her.

"What time is it?" she asked. The room was still quite dark.

"It's just after seven."

Caru groaned and closed her eyes again, snuggling back under the covers. "It's too early. We didn't get to bed til gone one remember?"

"But it's Christmas! Don't you normally get up early

on Christmas day? I always used to be up before dawn as a kid."

Caru sighed and peered at him, still struggling to open her eyes. "Yes, as a kid I used to get up early to see what Father Christmas had brought." She yawned. "But I was always in bed before nine back then."

Peter chuckled. "Sorry, I was just excited. I thought you might want to see what Father Christmas had brought you."

Caru frowned. "You already gave me my present yesterday. The nursery? Not to mention the little monster in my belly?"

Her stomach growled and they both laughed.

"Okay, well if you don't think you've been a good girl this year, I can send your gift back to the North Pole."

Caru shook her head and stretched her arms up above her head. "I'm awake! Maybe a cup of coffee would be a good idea though?"

Peter kissed her and nodded. "On it. See you downstairs."

Caru smiled at his child-like enthusiasm. She knew he would make a great father. She could imagine him making Christmases an elaborate affair for their child. He certainly knew how to make everything seem magical.

She felt her eyes closing, and had to pull the covers back for the cold air to hit her body to stay awake. Christmas day or not, she was definitely going to need a nap later.

She wrapped herself in her robe and put on some thick socks. She wandered over to their small en-suite and brushed her hair and her teeth, wanting to at least appear vaguely awake.

When she finally descended the wooden stairs that desperately needed some new carpet on them, she was greeted with the smell of coffee (decaf, but still smelled glorious) and cinnamon and something sweet she couldn't identify.

She entered the kitchen and stood in the doorway, watching Peter as he made them breakfast and hummed along to carols playing on the radio. When he turned to put two plates of waffles on the table, he saw her and grinned.

"Your breakfast is served, mia cara."

She grinned back, and sat down at the dining table, the smell of the waffles making her stomach growl again.

"Okay, okay little monster, I'll feed you now."

Peter sat opposite her and chuckled. You're going to end up calling our child Mike or Sully aren't you?"

Caru cut up her waffles and laughed. "Or how about Boo?"

Peter sipped his coffee and smiled at her. "Whatever we name him or her, they will be perfect."

Caru added a generous helping of maple syrup to her waffles, and savoured each mouthful. "You know, when I saw your waffle maker, I knew you were a keeper," she commented.

Peter sighed. "I knew it. I knew you were only staying with me for my culinary skills."

"Well duh," Caru teased. "Why else would I stay with you?"

He gave her a wounded look and she laughed.

Peter finished his breakfast quickly, and seemed in a hurry for her to finish hers, but she couldn't resist having a second course of fruit. Her little monster was hungry.

When she finally felt satisfied, and had another hot cup of coffee in hand, she followed Peter into the living room, smiling at his enthusiasm. He stood by the Christmas tree, and she scanned it for a gift, but didn't see anything different to the day before. Just the gifts underneath for his family, and the gifts she had bought him.

She frowned at him. "Am I supposed to be seeing something here?"

"Yes, close your eyes and it will appear."

Caru closed her eyes. She could hear the rustle of the tree branches. She had insisted on getting a real tree, despite the mess they made, because she wanted her child to grow up with the scent of a real Christmas tree to remind them of magic and wonder.

"Open your eyes," Peter said softly.

She opened her eyes and looked at the tree, but it looked the same, so she looked at Peter and gasped.

He was on one knee with a tiny box in his hand, bearing a ring that glittered in the twinkling lights on the tree.

"I know it's a bit cliché, getting you pregnant and having a quick wedding and all that, but the honest truth is that I have wanted to marry you from the moment I met you, and the only reason I didn't propose straight away is because I wasn't sure if marriage fit in with your plans for your life. And with me being away so much with work, it felt like too much to ask of you to keep waiting for me."

Caru's eyes were filling with tears as he spoke. He shifted slightly and took her hand.

"With all that in mind, Caru, would you do me the honour of being my wife? I promise to love and care for you, and our child, always, and always be the best version of myself that I can be for you."

Tears now freely flowing, Caru gripped his hand and nodded. "Yes."

Peter took the ring out of the box, and slipped it onto the ring finger of her left hand. But it got stuck on her knuckle. Peter frowned and tried to push it past.

"I guess my belly isn't the only thing that's swollen right now," she said with a chuckle.

"I swear I got the right size," he said, looking disappointed.

"I know you did. My hands are just swollen right now. We can get it resized in the New Year and then make our announcement." She pulled Peter up and he kissed her.

"I love you," he whispered.

"With all my heart," she whispered back, wondering where the words had come from.

Peter's eyes widened. "You haven't said that in months."

Caru smiled. "I was just waiting for the right moment."

"Nice healthy heartbeats."

Caru smiled up at Peter, then turned back to the radiologist, a little confused.

"Heartbeats?" she said, feeling her own speed up a little. "Mine and the baby's, or…?"

The radiologist smiled and pointed to two distinct shapes on the screen. "Yes, you're having twins."

Caru's eyes widened and she felt Peter's hand grip hers tightly. "What?"

She smiled at them both. "You're having twins."

Caru stared at the screen. Sure enough, there were two distinct shapes in the grainy image.

She gasped and looked up at Peter who looked as shocked as she felt. His eyes were wide too, staring at the screen.

"Are you sure you're not psychic?" she whispered, looking back at the screen. She could hear them, the two different heartbeats.

She was having twins.

An hour later, they were at home again, and Caru was sat at the dining table staring at the printout of the grainy black and white image.

"We could always wait a while to tell everyone, could cover us for birthday gifts too," Peter joked.

"I can't believe we're having two," Caru said. They had only just broken the news of her pregnancy yesterday to his family and they had been overjoyed. Perhaps even a little bit too excited. His mum had looked like she was about to have a heart attack. It was a good thing they hadn't told her about the shotgun wedding as well. But now, the idea of telling them there were going to be two babies…

"I better get that second crib," Peter mused as he made her a drink and got a packet of biscuits out of the cupboard.

She took one from him and nibbled on it without tasting it.

Would she be able to continue her business with twins? Did she want to be a working mum or a stay at home mum? She realised she would have to take a proper maternity leave now. Or maybe she could sell the business? The thought of having to let Becky go made her feel sad. There was so much to consider.

"Where are you?" Peter asked softly.

She looked up at him and smiled. "Just thinking of Time Traveller. I'm going to have to plan my maternity leave and eventual childcare, or sell and move on. I just don't see how it would be possible to continue with two little ones. Especially when you have to go on digs again. Even if they are still within the country."

Peter sighed. "Yeah, I hadn't thought about that. We'll need to organise child care if you choose to go back. Can't concentrate with babies in the office."

"I'll wait until New Year then start looking at options."

Peter nodded. "So shall we call everyone? Or just send them the photo and see if they work it out?"

Caru laughed. "Just send them the photo. I want to know if any of them will actually know what they are looking at because I wouldn't have had a clue without the radiologist's explanation."

Peter took a photo of the printout on his phone then sent it to his family. Caru did the same, and sent it to Becky and Jess. She frowned when she thought of Laura and wished she could send it to her too. But considering that they weren't close, and hadn't even spoken again since that one phone call weeks ago, it didn't seem appropriate. She couldn't wait to tell her mum. She just wished that she was still here to see her grandchildren.

They didn't have to wait long before their phones began to ping with messages from surprised family and friends about the two blobs on the photo.

But there was no reply from Jess. Caru was confused. She was sure that the scan photo would have got a reaction. She wondered if she should call, but then got distracted by Peter discussing how they would have to make changes in the nursery to fit two sets of everything in it.

By the time her mind returned to Jess, it was too late in the evening to call. She made a mental note to call her in the morning.

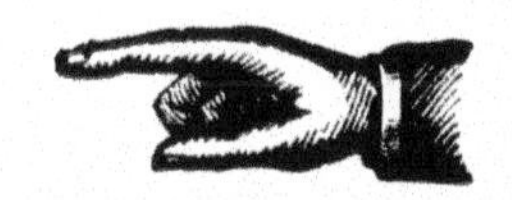

CHAPTER FIFTEEN

CARU shifted from one foot to the other, and rubbed her gloved hands together. It was bitterly cold. She wished she had kept a set of keys to her old flat rather than having to wait outside, pressing the buzzer.

She dialled Jess' number again, muttering expletives when her friend didn't pick up and the voicemail cut in.

"Jess, where are you?" she muttered. Maybe she should wait in the car with the heater on.

"Hi, Caru, you trying to get in?"

Caru turned at the sound of a familiar voice and saw her neighbour approaching from the garden.

"Hey, Mark. Yes, I was trying to get hold of Jess but she's not answering her phone or the door. Is she in?"

Mark raised an eyebrow. "Well considering the racket they were making this morning, I would say so."

Caru frowned. "Racket? What do you mean?"

Mark unlocked the door and let her into the foyer, which wasn't any warmer than outside. "Ever since that guy moved in they've done nothing but argue and shout. I have to admit it's beginning to drive me a bit crazy. Are you sure you don't want to move back in?"

Caru shivered and gave her old neighbour a half smile. "I'm sure. But that doesn't sound good. Thank you for letting me in."

Her neighbour nodded and she hurried up the stairs ahead of him, a growing feeling of dread in the pit of her stomach.

She reached the door to her old flat out of breath but only paused for a moment to rest before hammering on the wooden door.

"Jess?" she called out. She could hear some noise then the door cracked open a few inches. Her friend peered out into the hallway.

"Caru? How did you get in?"

"Mark let me in. Why didn't you answer your phone? Or the buzzer?"

"Oh, um, the buzzer isn't working properly. And my phone was on silent, sorry."

Caru raised an eyebrow. Her excuses were just a bit too rehearsed. Jess still wasn't opening the door fully, and Caru wasn't buying the story. "I need a pee. Can I come in? It's freezing out here."

"Oh, um, sure." Jess finally stepped back, opening the door wider, but stayed partially hidden behind the door while Caru stepped inside and made her way to the bathroom.

She was surprised to find the bathroom in a bit of a state. Jess normally kept things neat and tidy. She wondered if it was Henry creating the mess. She had only briefly met him before she moved out, and she hadn't been able to work out if she liked him or not. However, in that moment she knew that something was very wrong. Her intuition was screaming at her.

When she emerged, the front door was closed and she could hear movement in the kitchen. She found Jess filling the kettle. She looked around the open plan space, noting that despite what Jess had said on Christmas Eve, there were no decorations, no tree, in fact there was no sign of Christmas at all. Her intuition was now both screaming and waving a multitude of red flags. Jess adored Christmas. There was no way she wouldn't decorate and celebrate it. Something was very, very wrong.

She turned her attention to her friend. "Thanks, I find it hard to go for long these days. Can't imagine what it will be like when these two start growing." She waited for Jess to react to her words, but there was nothing. She frowned. "Jess? What's going on?"

When her housemate finally turned around to face her, she couldn't help the gasp that escaped from her lips.

Jess's eye was swollen and purple, and there was a line of bruises at the base of her neck, and a cut on her lip.

"Jess! What the hell happened?"

"It's nothing," Jess muttered. "Keep your voice down."

"The hell it's nothing," Caru said in a lower tone, moving toward her housemate to see the damage up close. She listened out for movement in the flat. "Henry?" she whispered.

Jess nodded slightly as the kettle began to boil. Caru's blood was boiling along with the water and she had to breathe deeply and stop herself from marching into his room and demanding to know what the hell he had done to her friend.

Caru wasn't afraid of him but she was afraid of what further damage he could do if she angered him. She breathed in deeply, trying to stay calm.

"Jess, he's got to go," she hissed, trying to keep her voice down. "This is not acceptable, even if it was the first time?"

"It's not the first time," Jess muttered, Caru could barely hear her over the noise of the kettle. She pushed her sleeves up and Caru could see the faded bruises in the shape of handprints.

Caru began to shake, partially with shock and partially with rage. "I'm calling the police, right now." She began to dig into her handbag.

"No!" Jess said, grabbing Caru's arm. "They won't do anything, and besides, it's not his fault, he just gets very passionate about things, and can't help himself."

Caru shook her head. "Jess, this is NOT passion. This is violence, pure and simple, and he needs to be stopped. Look at you!" Her voice was raising and she took another deep breath to try to calm herself. She studied her friend's appearance. "You've lost weight too? Are you eating properly?"

Jess shook her head. "He doesn't like me going out. Gets jealous of the checkout guys at the supermarket."

"Pack your things. If you won't call the police, you're coming with me." Caru's hormones were kicking into overdrive, and she knew if she didn't leave soon, her mama bear mode would take over and she wouldn't be able to stop herself from teaching Henry not to touch her friend.

"I can't," Jess said. "Please, just go, I can handle him,

it's okay."

"Jess, it is NOT okay. Just grab the important stuff, you can borrow my clothes. Come stay with me and Peter."

Caru heard footsteps in the hall behind her and her heartbeat quickened, her hands reflexively balled up into fists.

"Hey, is lunch ready yet?"

Caru bristled at the sound of Henry's voice behind her, and she turned to face him, her anger barely restrained beneath the surface.

Henry saw her and raised an eyebrow. "Oh, Cassie, right?"

"Caru," Caru said, correcting him.

"Yeah that's what I said. Babe, lunch?" He went over to Jess and wrapped his arm around her waist and Caru saw Jess flinch. In that moment, something snapped inside her, and she took a step back.

"I have to go," she said. "I'll see myself out."

Jess frowned but nodded, and Henry ignored her completely.

She backed away and headed to the door, but on her way she quietly grabbed the spare set of keys from the hook by the door. She closed the flat door behind her and then went downstairs so that she was out of earshot. Then she got her phone out and called the police.

By the time Caru got home that evening, she felt as though she had aged ten years.

Peter was waiting for her with dinner cooked and his

arms open to engulf her in a hug. She had called him after calling the police to explain what was going on.

"How is Jess?" he asked, holding her tightly.

"She will be okay, I hope. But Peter, she was so broken. I've never seen her like that."

Peter kissed her, then guided her to a chair at the table and set a cup of tea in front of her.

"It wasn't just the physical harm. She just seemed lifeless. Her spirit was gone." Caru's voice cracked and as the adrenalin finally wore off, the events of the day caught up with her.

Peter knelt beside her chair, his arms around her while she rested her head on his shoulder and cried for her friend. Her beautiful, strong-willed friend, who had been reduced to the wreck she was now.

"Henry was taken into custody, but it's supposedly his first offence, so it's not likely to go far. I helped Jess pack up his stuff and put it outside the building. I notified the neighbours so they know not to let him in, but it's likely that Jess will have to move."

"It might be the most sensible thing to do," Peter agreed. "Men like that, they often don't give up that easily."

Caru sighed. "I keep wondering if I did the right thing. What if I've just made it worse?"

Peter shook his head and touched her wet cheek. "You did the right thing. How could you have left her there with him? After seeing what he had done?"

Caru nodded and wiped her face with the napkin. "I know, it's just so tricky. I wish Jess had come home with me. I begged her to but she was insistent that she was okay."

Peter sat opposite her and poured himself some wine. "All you can do is check in on her. Hopefully, he will get some help and never do that to another woman."

Caru sighed. "I do hope so. I just feel so bad. If I hadn't moved out, he wouldn't have moved in, and this wouldn't have happened."

Peter frowned. "You can't feel bad for living your life. It's not your responsibility to keep everyone you know safe and happy."

Caru nodded. "I know. It just hurt to see Jess like that." Peter served up their dinner. She wasn't very hungry after the day's events, but knew that she needed to eat, otherwise the twins would keep her awake.

She ate a few mouthfuls of pasta then tried to smile at Peter. But she knew that he wasn't fooled.

CHAPTER SIXTEEN

"HAPPY New Year, my love."

Caru smiled at Peter and they kissed. They had opted for a low key celebration in light of her lack of energy and the drama of the past few days. So they were curled up on the sofa watching movies and eating a box of chocolates left over from Christmas.

"Happy New Year," Caru replied. She sighed. "What a year it's been. I am literally not the same person I was at the beginning of last year."

"You have changed," Peter agreed.

Caru looked at him curiously. "What would you say was different about me?"

Peter was thoughtful for a moment. "You're more emotional, I guess. Though that could be the hormones? You seem a little more scattered, unsure at times. You were always so confident, so focused on your business, and on reaching your goals. But when I got back from the dig you were different. More open, more vulnerable. More concerned about others, about their happiness."

Caru bit her lip. "Is that a bad thing?"

Peter chuckled. "No, of course not. It's just different." He kissed her forehead. "I like the new you. I wouldn't have asked you to marry me if I didn't."

Caru smiled, "Good. Don't think I've gone too soft though, there's still a fierceness inside me. That much became clear this week."

"Oh yeah," Peter agreed. "I wouldn't mess with you, that's for certain."

Caru giggled and snuggled tighter to his side. "Let's hope this next year is a better one for us all." Peter murmured in agreement as their attention turned back to the TV. Caru thought of Jess, and hoped that her friend managed to enjoy celebrating the New Year. She had spoken to her earlier in the day and she had sounded more positive. She was looking for a new place to live, mainly because the flat held too many painful memories, but also because there was the possibility that Henry might try to return. She was meeting some friends to celebrate with that evening, and she had sounded excited, and much more like her old self. And her friend Kate was going to come and stay at the flat with her in the next couple of days to help her pack and so that she wasn't alone.

Caru was looking forward to helping her friend move, to create her new home, to begin again. She just hoped Jess would regain her strength and vibrance in time.

"Caru?"

Caru blinked and looked around, smiling when she saw Charlie sat on the step, the sunlight making him squint up at her.

"Charlie! Are you okay?"

"Oh, Caru, I wish it was as simple as that."

Caru frowned. "What do you mean?"

Charlie shook his head then turned his attention to her left. Caru turned to look and saw Jess walking towards her.

"Jess! What are you doing here?"

Jess stopped a few feet away and smiled at Caru. "I came to tell you it's not your fault, and that you have been an amazing friend to me."

Caru frowned. "What? What's not my fault? Jess? What's going on?"

Jess went over to Charlie and sat next to him on the step. "It's okay, Charlie will look after me now. I'm just sorry I never got to meet your babies, or come to your wedding."

Caru's eyes grew wide and panic overwhelmed her. "What are you talking about? How do you know about the wedding? We haven't told anyone yet. Not even Peter's family. And Charlie is dead. But you, no, you're not, Jess!"

"Caru!"

Caru woke with a gasp, and found Peter touching her shoulder, standing by the bed. "Your phone was ringing downstairs, so I went to get it."

Caru blinked rapidly, trying to wake up. She took the phone from Peter and peered at the bright screen. The clock said 4.36am. She unlocked it and saw missed calls from Jess at 1am. Then at 3am, three missed calls from her old neighbour, Mark.

Hands shaking, she called Jess, but there was no reply. So she rang Mark's number, and Peter sat next to her, his arm around her shoulders while it rang. She put it on speakerphone.

"Caru?"

"Mark, what's wrong? I missed your calls."

Mark sighed heavily down the phone. "Oh, Caru, I'm so sorry to call in the middle of the night, but it's Jess. She met some friends in town tonight but it seems that Henry followed her back and managed to get into the flat."

Caru felt like her heart had stopped as she waited for her neighbour to continue.

"I heard a commotion and went up to see what was going on. I called the police as soon as I realised, but I was too late."

Caru's heart thudded. "Too late?" she whispered. Peter gripped her hand tightly.

"He killed her, Caru," he said, his voice shaking. "She was already gone by the time we broke the door down. He escaped down the fire escape. The police are searching for him now."

Caru gasped and her hand flew to her mouth. "What?" she sputtered.

"I'm so sorry, Caru," Mark said.

Caru's vision blurred and she started to shake.

"Mark, this is Peter. Do we need to do anything? Is she... still there?"

"No, an ambulance took her away, and I've locked up the flat. Obviously the police will need access tomorrow, but I can sort that. Hopefully they will find the evil bastard and lock him up."

Caru's whole body was shaking with silent sobs while she listened to the men talk for a few moments, then she tried to utter a goodbye to her neighbour but couldn't get the words out. Peter said it for her and hung up the phone.

"What have I done?" she gasped. Her friend. Her beautiful, talented, vibrant friend. Gone.

Her dream came back to her in a rush and she saw Jess sitting in the sunshine on the step with Charlie.

"He'll look after me now."

The sobs tore through her body and despite Peter's calming embrace, Caru couldn't stop.

Her friend was dead, and it was all her fault. No matter what Jess had said in her dream. Caru was the one who had moved out. She was the one who had involved the police and angered Henry. And now her friend was dead because of her.

Three days after Jess's funeral, Caru was sat at the dining table, a cold cup of tea in front of her, her gaze fixed on the crack in the wall, which she absentmindedly thought someone really should fix.

"Caru, I need to go to work, but I'm worried about you."

She pulled her gaze up and to the left to look at Peter. She nodded, but her gaze didn't properly focus on his face, and she knew he could tell.

"It's okay, go to work," she said, hearing the lack of energy in her voice. "I'll be fine."

She could see he wasn't convinced, and she couldn't

blame him, she wasn't even convincing herself.

Peter kissed her on the head, and squeezed her shoulder, but she didn't even hear the front door opening and closing, or the sound of his car pulling out of the driveway.

She just kept going over and over what happened after Christmas, and then New Years', and then at the funeral. If only Jess had come to stay with her. If only Jess' friend, Kate, could have come to stay straight away. If only she had never moved out in the first place. If only.

It still just didn't feel real that Jess was really gone. After her breakdown the night she died, Caru had been unable to cry. She must have looked like such a cold bitch at the service to Jess' other friends and family. She just sat there with no expression, staring at the wooden box that held the body of a woman who had so much life left to live.

It just wasn't right.

Henry was still out there somewhere too. The police hadn't managed to track him down. What if he did it again?

Over and over, she wondered how she should have handled the situation. How she could have protected Jess. How she could have prevented her death.

But she had no idea how she could have done it differently. Henry was dangerous. And even if she hadn't set off the chain of events now, the likelihood was that he would have ended up killing Jess eventually anyway.

The only way to have protected her was if she had never met him in the first place. But that was impossible. Despite the name of her business, time travel wasn't actually possible.

Moving to another reality apparently was though.

Caru sipped her cold tea and didn't even notice the rancid taste of the curdled milk.

She didn't even know if it was possible to go back. If her old life even existed anymore. And there was no one she could ask, not without getting committed. Besides, even if she could go back, how could she leave Peter? They would never have met in her old life so she wouldn't be living with him, or be getting married, or be pregnant with twins.

She pushed the thought away. She couldn't go back. As much as she wanted her friend back, and Charlie back, and her friendship with Laura and her children back; the idea of returning to the struggle, the overwhelm and the loneliness was too much. She needed to put her own happiness first.

Even though, in that moment, she couldn't imagine being happy ever again.

"Good morning," Caru said to Becky as she entered the agency. It was a very damp January so far, but Caru was far too hot in her raincoat. She felt like she needed another shower.

"Morning," Becky replied. "How are you doing?"

Caru shrugged her coat off, and nodded to her employee. "Not too bad, as long as I don't stop too long to think." It felt too soon to be back at work, but she was going stir-crazy at home alone, staring at the walls, agonising over her decisions and actions. She needed distractions.

Becky took her coat from her to hang up and sighed. "Still can't quite believe it all, I hope they find him and lock him away for good."

Caru sat at her desk and did her best to reign in both her tears and her anger. "Me too."

Becky started the coffee machine, which Caru had bought for Christmas after their old one broke. "Decaf?" she asked Caru.

"Please. Though today I really am missing the caffeine," she replied, yawning.

"Still having nightmares?" Becky asked, placing the steaming cup in front of her.

Caru sighed. "They're not really nightmares, just really vivid dreams. Sometimes they're so real, I get confused when I wake up."

"Wish I could remember my dreams," Becky said. "But they always slip away before I can recall them."

Caru sipped the coffee and winced. The new coffee machine seemed to make it far hotter than it needed to be. She set it down, and got her laptop out and signed into her email. After New Year, she had taken a week off to help with Jess's funeral and try to compose herself, but work had piled up and even though she had worked from home for a few days, she still hadn't managed to clear her emails. There had been an earthquake in one of their popular holiday destinations, which had screwed up some of their reservations as the hotels were now damaged, so she had a lot of concerned customers emailing to ask what the new plans were.

She took a deep breath and focused on the issues on her screen, determined to make it through the day without needing to hide in the bathroom, her heart racing, eyes stinging with unshed tears, her body shaking with grief.

She picked the trickiest email to tackle first, and lost herself in the world of travel reservations, as banal and trivial as they seemed to be in that moment.

In no time at all it was lunchtime, and Becky went to pick up their regular lunch order, which was now a cheese salad baguette, as onions still seemed to turn Caru's stomach.

"Becky, how would you feel about taking on a more prominent role in the business?" she asked her employee, while they ate.

Becky swallowed her mouthful of sandwich quickly and gulped some water. "What do you mean?"

Caru sighed. "I'm trying to make a long-term plan for the business, because once these two arrive," she said, gesturing to her stomach. "I just don't think I'll be able to keep up with everything. And though I've considered selling the business, it doesn't feel right. I want to keep it going, but I can't just dump everything on you, it wouldn't be fair. So I've been thinking of hiring a new you, and you could step into my role, at least for the first six months or so, and then we can review from there. I could still do a few things from home to keep things running smoothly, but the daily operations would be entirely down to you."

Becky's eyes were wide, but in excitement, not fear, as Caru had hoped.

"I would love that! Are you serious? You know how much I love this place, and how much overtime I've done."

Caru smiled. "It hasn't gone unnoticed. Your Spring Bonus will be a decent one, I promise. And, of course, there would be a pay rise if you took on the role. I have done the figures, and I think I can afford to do that while hiring a new team member. I'll need your help to find someone, because you will be the one working with them."

Becky nodded. "I'll get started on creating the job ad straight away!"

Caru chuckled. "Finish your lunch first, then we can figure out how to find your clone." She chewed another mouthful of her baguette. "Thank you, Becky. For everything. You really are a wonderful employee and friend. And now, partner."

Becky jumped up and gave Caru a hug. "Thank you! I won't let you down, I promise."

Caru hugged her back. "I know you won't."

Becky sat back down, bouncing up and down in her chair, clearly too excited to eat.

"Is there anything else you need me to do today?"

Caru shook her head. "No, but I do need to nip out to the jewellers, if you can man the fort while I do that."

Becky nodded. "Getting anything nice?"

Caru smiled. "Just getting something adjusted, a Christmas gift."

"Oh great. Well, I'm going to get back to these emails, shall we go over the advert this afternoon?"

"Yes, no time like the present." Caru finished her lunch and threw the wrapper away. She picked up her handbag and then put on her raincoat. "I'll be back in five."

"No rush," Becky replied.

CHAPTER SEVENTEEN

"YOU'RE leaving early?"

Caru smiled at Peter over the table at breakfast the next morning. "Yeah, I thought I'd look in the craft shop in town before work. I never did get a chance to pick up any wool, and I'd really love to make something for the twins."

Peter smiled and kissed her. "Still can't believe you can knit. Never seen you make anything except a mess in the kitchen since we met."

Caru chuckled but felt sad inside. How was it possible that she wasn't at all creative in this life? Her mind flashed back to her beloved printing press, her art supplies, knitting, and even jewellery making. In her other life, she hadn't gone a single day without making something. The last few months had been a weird experience for the creative in her. But in a strange way, her old way of life felt distant and hazy, and despite the lack of creativity, she still had a sense of fulfilment. In fact, when she thought about buying craft supplies, she didn't have the feeling of excitement and anticipation she'd had previously. The compulsion to fill her time and space had gone. Completely. She frowned. Why was that? Aware that Peter was observing her as these thoughts flew around her head, she smiled at him.

"Hopefully I can remember how to, after all this time," she said, picking up her handbag. "I'll pick up the ring too, then we can finally tell everyone. I have nearly done so by accident a few times now." She smiled at Peter as he spilled cornflakes on the floor in his bid to finish his breakfast quickly. "Are you off now too?"

Peter nodded and swallowed the last spoonful of cereal. "Yep, I'll see you later." He put his bowl by the sink, kissed her one more time. "You look fabulous today, by the way."

Caru glanced down at her black dress. She looked the same as she always did, her wardrobe still mostly consisted of black and navy clothing. She smiled up at Peter and he gave her a cute grin before dashing out the door.

Caru rested a hand on her stomach. How had she got so lucky? Perhaps it wasn't so much luck, perhaps it was simply that she had taken a different fork in the road, and ended up somewhere entirely different. She stood for a moment, and went within, to find stillness, and peace. She felt whole. Complete. With no need to fill her life with things she loved because her life was already so completely full of love. Tears prickled her eyes, and she breathed in deeply. She had never consciously felt like this before and she wanted to remember it.

Aware that she was going to be late if she lingered any further, she got her coat, slipped it on and headed to the door. She couldn't wait until she got her ring back from the jewellers so they could tell everyone their exciting news. They had said when she dropped it off it would be ready to collect the next day, so she would pick it up in her lunch break.

Caru locked the front door, and went to her pink Mini. She got in and turned the key, but nothing happened. She frowned and tried again, but there was just a click and then silence. The battery was dead.

Muttering curses about how annoying it was that she couldn't have realised the battery was dead just a few minutes earlier and got a jump start from Peter, she picked up her bag, got out of the car and locked the door. So much for getting into town early, now she would have to get the bus, and who knew how long that would take?

She walked to the bus stop at the end of the lane, thanking the gods for it being a dry day. When she got there, she wrapped her scarf a bit tighter around her neck and face. It was very mild for the end of January, but the dress still wasn't really the best attire for hanging around at the bus stop. She should have worn trousers.

Twenty minutes later, the bus rolled up, and Caru was grateful to get inside in the warmth. She smiled at the bus driver and put her change into the box.

The bus was quite empty, just a man at the back and an older lady sitting at the front. She chose a seat in the middle and sat down heavily. She still wasn't showing much, but she had already put on six pounds since December, and it felt like much more.

The bus rattled away from the stop, heading the long

way into town, around the country lanes. She glanced at her phone, thinking she should warn Becky she might be late, when she noticed the date.

It was Jess' birthday.

A lump blocked her throat and she choked, a flood of unshed tears stinging her eyes.

She closed her eyes and thought back to Jess' last birthday. She had thrown her a surprise dinner party, inviting her friends and work colleagues, and decorating the flat. Jess had said it was the best birthday she'd ever had.

For the first time since New Years', the tears streamed down Caru's face. Oh how she wished her friend was still alive. She missed her so much. It just wasn't fair that she was gone. She closed her eyes and leaned her head against the back of the seat.

'I'm so, so sorry, Jess,' she thought. 'I wish I could change things, I wish you were still here with me. I love you.'

The sound of the bell trilling and the vehicle coming to an abrupt halt jolted Caru and she opened her eyes, feeling like she had woken up from an odd nap. She got up and lurched to the front of the bus, her body feeling stiff and achy.

She smiled at the bus driver and thanked him.

"Welcome back," he replied.

She frowned. What an odd thing to say. Shaking her head, she headed to the top of town, skipping the craft shop in favour of grabbing a coffee instead, before getting to work in just the nick of time.

She stepped into the coffee shop, a little out of breath, and headed straight to the counter, thankful that there was no queue.

Before she could utter a word, the barista nodded. "The usual?"

Caru nodded. She'd had enough decafs in December for them to become the new usual, so she trusted that she didn't need to remind her. She headed to the other end of the counter to wait for her order, and instead of scrolling through her Instagram, she took the few minutes to breathe deeply. She decided to light a candle later, in Jess' memory. And then on the weekend, she would go and visit her grave. It was in the same cemetery as her mum, she could visit them both. Tears threatened again, but she closed her eyes and breathed deeply again, maintaining her composure.

"Order for Carrie!"

Caru opened her eyes and saw the two paper cups on the counter bearing her name with the wrong spelling.

She frowned. "I only ordered one decaf?"

The barista shook her head. "No, you order a tea and a coffee. Every morning. You have for over a year now."

Caru picked up the cups, the heat of them seeping into her palms. "Oh," she said, wondering if she was dreaming again. They really were getting stupidly vivid. Soon, she would have no idea when she was dreaming or awake.

The door opened as a customer entered, and the notes of a guitar and a soulful voice wafted in with them on the breeze and she smiled.

Charlie. This was definitely a dream. She nodded to the barista and headed out the door, pausing for a moment to listen to Charlie as he strummed away, his eyes closed.

When the last note faded she spoke.

"Hey," she said.

Charlie's eyes opened and when he saw her, his whole face lit up. Caru's heart leapt. It was so good to see him smile. In her last few dreams, he had been so sad.

She held out the tea to him, and he took it, placing it on the step next to him.

"I had a dream about you," he said, looking up at her.

Caru smiled. "Really? What happened?"

Charlie was quiet for a moment. "I wrote a song about it, would you like to hear it?"

For some reason, Caru felt like this would be a moment she would want to remember forever. "Yes, I'd love to." She pulled her phone out of her bag. "Can I record it?" It seemed like a bit of a pointless thing to do, considering she was dreaming, but she felt that maybe it would help her to remember more of it when she woke up.

Charlie nodded, and she crouched down, placed her coffee on the pavement in front of her, and then opened the camera app.

She hit the record button, and Charlie began to strum softly. She resisted the urge to close her eyes, afraid she might wake up and miss the song. She watched him intently as he began to sing.

"Every day I sit here, come rain or shine,
People hurry by me and they don't see me falling.
Some days it's hard to keep just sitting here,
That is until she comes along and brings me

Faith in a teacup,
Hope in a sincere smile
Love in a greeting,
Makes life feel worthwhile

Most people live for the weekend, but no, not me
I live for Monday mornings,
When I look up and see
Her smiling back at me
Every day I try to tell her, what she means to me,
But the words stick in my throat
And all I can do is accept her

Faith in a teacup,
Hope in a sincere smile,
Love in a greeting,
Makes my life worthwhile.

I had a dream last night that
She went away
And my Monday morning was so
Cold and grey
That I climbed to the top of the ridge
And left this world
Because the only thing keeping me here was

Faith in a teacup
Hope in a sincere smile,
Love in a greeting,
It's all that makes life worthwhile

When I woke up this morning
I knew I had to
Write this song
To tell this girl how I've
Felt all along
I'm sure she had no idea how much it meant to me

That my whole world revolved around
Her and that cup of tea

Faith in a teacup
Hope in a sincere smile,
Love in a greeting,
Makes life worthwhile.
You make life worthwhile."

Caru's hands were shaking slightly, and tears were streaming down her cheeks. Charlie had opened his eyes for the final line, and he was staring at her.

"That was beautiful," she whispered, aware that a crowd had gathered, but unable to tear her gaze from his. She wished this wasn't a dream so that she could watch Charlie singing the song again and again.

He lowered his guitar a little and sighed. "It wasn't a dream was it?"

Caru pressed stop on her phone and put it in her bag. She frowned. "What do you mean?"

"You left. And I left. And someone else left, a girl with dark hair, but I don't know her name. She was in the dream too."

"Jess," Caru said. "Wait, I'm dreaming right now though, aren't I?"

Charlie smiled crookedly and picked up his cup. "This tea feels pretty real to me."

Caru frowned and pulled her phone back out of her bag and looked at the time and date. It was 10.05am, so she was late for work. But the date was... hang on. It was Jess' birthday. The 29th January 2020. But her phone said it was September 28th.

2019.

Caru blinked rapidly. The odd words of the bus driver came back to her.

"Welcome back."

Her heart thudded and she gasped. "I'm, I'm back?" She stood up, her legs quivering, her vision greying at the edges.

She unlocked her phone and scrolled through to Jess's number. She hit the green button, and tried to calm her breathing while it rang.

"Hello?"

At the sound of Jess' voice, Caru gulped in another breath. "Jess!" she squeaked. "You're okay!"

"Caru? Of course I'm okay, I just decided to work from home today. Are you okay? You sound weird."

"I'm good, I'm good," Caru squeezed out, feeling like she couldn't get enough air into her lungs. "Was just checking, I'll um, see you later. I love you."

"I love you too," Jess replied with a chuckle. "See you later."

Eyes wide, Caru hung up and looked at Charlie.

"She's okay," she whispered, before the world went black.

CHAPTER EIGHTEEN

"CARU? Caru, can you hear me?"

"Peter?" Caru whispered as she woke to a familiar voice. For a moment, relief flooded her body. She was safe, at home, and she would open her eyes and see Peter looking at her in concern, after having had a very realistic dream. He would hold her while she cried, then they would have breakfast together.

"Caru? It's Kevin, open your eyes, darl'."

Caru's eyes flew open. The familiar voice did indeed belong to her former friend and boss.

"Kevin?"

He smiled, but his bright blue eyes still looked concerned. "Forgot to eat breakfast? Not known you to pass out before."

She looked around to see that she was in the art gallery. Her gaze focused on another figure nearby.

"Charlie?"

"He carried you here. When you passed out in the street. Good thing too, it's cold out there. He wanted to call an ambulance but didn't have a phone and couldn't unlock yours. But I can take you to A&E now if you still feel off?"

Caru blinked rapidly, as her mind raced with the implications of this not being a dream. She saw a stand in the corner of the room, holding her greeting cards.

"Kevin, when did I see you last?"

Kevin chuckled uncomfortably. "Well, I know I haven't been around much, but I promise to be here more. I've just been distracted."

Caru shook her head. "It wasn't a criticism. Just a question." She sat up, feeling bruised and achy from her fall. She let Kevin help her into a chair.

"Well, in that case, it was a week ago. We had a meeting about the Christmas exhibition?"

Caru nodded, searching her memory of her old life for that meeting. "It starts on the 1st November," she said, remembering their discussion.

"Yeah, which doesn't give us much time to plan. That's why I'm here this morning actually. I was hoping we could go through it. But that's probably not the best idea."

Caru shook her head. She was still trying to recalibrate back to her old reality. She worked at the gallery. She made things. Charlie was alive. Jess was alive.

Peter...

"Where's my phone?" she asked, her heart beginning to thump painfully.

Charlie pulled it out of his pocket and handed it to her. He was being oddly quiet.

She saw that the corner of the screen was cracked,

probably from her fall onto the concrete pavement. Ignoring that, she opened the phone and went straight to the text messages. She scrolled through but didn't see any from Peter. She opened her contacts, but his number was not there.

She hadn't thought to memorise it.

Silently cursing him for being averse to social media, and therefore most likely untraceable, she opened her last messages to Jess, and was upset but not surprised to see no sign of the scan photo. Because of course, if she hadn't met Peter then she wouldn't be pregnant with twins right now either. Her hand went to her flat stomach, and a sob rose in her throat.

Her perfect life was gone. Her new family was gone. Which meant that her new home, her business, and even her car, were also gone.

Trying not to completely break down in front of Kevin, who was now busy doing paperwork, she looked up to see Charlie watching her intently.

"Thank you for bringing me here, Charlie."

He nodded. "I should go rescue my guitar. Not that anyone would steal it."

Caru nodded. "I'll see you tomorrow?"

Charlie smiled. "I'd like that."

He left, and she got up and went to the stand bearing her creations. She picked up one of her favourite designs and smoothed her finger over the impression of the phrase she had so carefully inked.

"Did you want to go to hospital? Or home?"

She looked at Kevin. Her friend whom she had missed over the last few months, even if she hadn't realised it.

"I'd like to go home."

♥ ♥ ♥

Caru hadn't said a word in the car on the way to her flat, but Kevin seemed happy to drive in silence. In truth, it wasn't because Caru had nothing to say, but because there was too much.

She was barely able to make sense of it all, so she certainly didn't expect anyone else to be able to.

When they pulled up outside her home, she looked up at the old building, memories of trying to save Jess from Henry, and failing, flooding her mind. She took a deep breath and looked at Kevin.

"Thank you. I'm sorry I messed things up."

Kevin chuckled. "You haven't messed anything up, but you clearly need to take some time off. I've been working you too hard. Take the next few days, and I'll see you on Saturday, ok?"

Caru nodded, grateful to have him as her boss and friend.

"Thank you for the ride." She got out of the car, and slammed the door shut. She dug around in her bag and found her keys, finding it strange that they contained her flat key, but not her business, car or new home keys. They felt too light as she slotted the key into the lock on the main door.

She stepped into the foyer, and checked the mail, but there was nothing but takeout menus and other junk. She put it all straight into the recycling bin, then headed up the wide stairs, trying to breathe normally, but finding her emotions rising up and threatening her with more tears.

She reached the flat door, slightly out of breath from

ascending the two flights, and shakily put the key in the lock.

When she stepped into the flat, she could smell Jess' favourite scented candle, and the tears began to fall. She followed her nose to the kitchen, and set her handbag on the stool. The kitchen and lounge were empty.

"Hey, what are you doing home?"

Caru turned to see her housemate, her beautiful friend, and couldn't stop herself from rushing to her and engulfing her in a bear hug.

Confused, Jess hugged her back, and though she tried to pull back a couple of times, Caru couldn't loosen her grip.

When her tears had slowed, Caru finally loosened her embrace, but still didn't let Jess go.

"What's going on?" Jess asked, her confusion plainly on her face.

"Please don't date anyone named Henry," Caru choked out.

Jess laughed and wriggled out of her grasp, heading to put the kettle on. "Pretty odd request, but okay. What's going on? Why are you crying?"

Caru wanted so desperately to tell her everything. About the different reality she had found herself in for several months. About Charlie, about Peter, her home, her business, her engagement, her pregnancy, but then that would mean telling Jess about her own demise, and who would want to hear that?

"Nothing, it's just been a weird day. I had a bit of a strange turn, so Kevin insisted on bringing me home."

"Strange turn? Are you okay?" Jess asked, her confusion becoming concern.

"Yeah, I think I just didn't eat enough this morning. Low blood sugar."

"You do tend to get a bit hangry when you've not eaten," Jess agreed. "Shall I make us some early lunch? I need a break anyway."

Caru nodded. "I'll just go get changed."

Jess smiled and started assembling ingredients for their usual sandwiches.

Caru picked up her handbag and went to her room, and for a moment, when she opened her door, she expected to see the minimal space that she had become used to.

The cluttered, untidy sight that greeted her was a shock, even though by now she was fully expecting that everything had reverted to how it once was.

She dumped her bag on her messy desk, and took off her coat and scarf. She added them to the pile of clothing on her desk chair and made her way to her almost empty wardrobe. She sighed. Every item of clothing was either discarded on the floor, or in the wash bin. She sifted through the piles on the floor until she found a favourite jumper and some soft pyjama bottoms. She took off her black dress, slipped the pyjamas on, and brushed her hair.

When she felt more comfortable, she surveyed the room again. Her gaze settled on her printing press. Despite having everything she'd ever wanted in the other reality, and despite feeling complete, there was still a part of her that had missed being creative. Making things with paper, ink, yarn, thread, fabric, metal.

She ran a hand over the type that was still set in the chase from the last batch of cards she had printed. Though she remembered printing them a few days before, it also felt like a whole lifetime before.

Which in a way, it was.

She hoped that her creativity might help her to process what she had just experienced. Because she didn't think it would be possible to talk to anyone about it. It was just too strange and unreal. Her mum popped into her mind, and she decided to visit her soon. No doubt her grave would be wild and untended, which was unacceptable to her now.

She left her room, tripping up on some clothes as she did. She made a mental note to have a good sort out. Though she was pleased to have all of her things back, she had really enjoyed having some clear space to be able to think in. She felt like the stuff she had accumulated had been a substitute for the love and connection she had craved. If she could just remember the feeling of being loved, remember the words in those letters, remember how it felt to be held by Peter, then maybe she could bring elements of her other life into her current existence.

If only Peter had been on Facebook, she could have found him and got in touch to see if they could ignite the spark they had shared. But for all she knew, in this reality he could be with someone else, in some faraway place or even dead.

Pushing the awful thought away, Caru joined Jess in the kitchen and ate lunch with her friend, thankful to at least have reversed the tragic fate of such a beautiful woman. The world needed Jess, and Charlie, and Laura's children. So she would have to find a way to be okay without Peter.

CHAPTER NINETEEN

"CARU! What are you doing here?"

Caru didn't answer, she just dropped her bags on the step and threw her arms around her best friend. She could hear the sounds of the children in another room as they played. She could hear a football commentator on the TV in the lounge and knew that Rob would be watching intently.

She gripped Laura, trying her best not to cry. Of everyone she had lost in the other reality, she had missed Laura the most. She hadn't realised how much they had drifted apart, and how much she had taken her for granted, until she was no longer there.

Her breathing was ragged and she could feel the concern in her friend's grip.

"What's wrong?" Laura whispered into her shoulder, the fear in her voice palpable.

She pulled back and looked into Laura's eyes, which

were tired and wrinkled at the edges from too many sleepless nights thanks to the three gorgeous children in the other room.

"I missed you," Caru said. Unable to stop them, tears filled her eyes.

This was why she hadn't been happy. This was the cause of the feeling of emptiness she had experienced in her perfect life. She had missed her closest friend.

Laura was frowning, her own eyes filling in empathetic response. "Caru, you're scaring me, what's wrong?"

Caru shook her head. "Nothing." She tried to smile. "Can I come in?"

"Of course," Laura grabbed Caru's smaller bag, and Caru picked up her rucksack and followed her friend into the familiar chaos of her cosy home.

"Rob!" Laura called out. "Caru is here."

"Hi, Caru!" Rob called out, not moving from his seat in front of the TV. Laura rolled her eyes and shook her head, Caru smiled.

"Glad to see some things haven't changed," Caru said.

"You were only here the other week, of course nothing has changed." Laura put the kettle on and got three mugs out. She looked at Caru. "Though it feels like everything has changed? You're different, but I don't know why. Are you sure nothing's wrong? You're not ill or something?"

Caru plucked an apple from the fruit bowl. She was hungry and hadn't packed enough food for the train journey there.

"I'm not ill," she said, knowing that her friend knew her too well to be blown off by a vague explanation. "But everything is different."

Laura frowned and poured hot water onto the tea bags

while Caru cut chunks off the apple with a sharp knife and ate them. Laura picked up one of the mugs and left the kitchen, presumably to take it to Rob.

"Caru!"

She looked to the door and smiled when she saw little Harriet standing there, jam smeared around her mouth, green felt tip pen all over her hands and t-shirt.

"Hey, little monster," she said, putting the knife and apple down on the counter and opening her arms. Harriet grinned and ran to her, and when she picked her up and hugged her small body to hers, more tears threatened. Despite her lack of maternal urges previously, being pregnant had changed that. Feeling loved by her own parents had changed that. She wondered what the twins would have looked like. Would they have had Peter's eyes? Her hair? Peter's cheeky smile?

"Why sad?" Harriet asked, touching Caru's wet cheek. Caru smiled at her. "Just happy to see you," she said, but it was only partly true.

Harriet gave her a sloppy kiss on the cheek and Caru kissed her cheek in return. "Love you," she said.

Caru's heart ached. "Love you too," she echoed.

Harriet wriggled in her embrace so Caru set her down, where she promptly ran off to re-join her siblings.

Caru followed her, and watched from the doorway as Harriet and Joy played with dolls on the floor, while Mary slept contentedly in her bouncer.

"Shall we go into the sunroom?" Laura asked, coming up behind her. "Rob will keep an eye on the kids."

Though Caru doubted Rob's ability to leave the TV screen if needed, she needed to talk to her friend desperately, so she nodded and followed her back to the kitchen to get their cups of tea and a packet of biscuits, then followed her out to the relative calm of the sunroom.

It had been a clear day, so the room was cosy and warm. In the summer it was unbearably hot in there, and in the winter, freezing cold. Spring and autumn were the only times it was a useable space.

Caru settled on the wicker sofa, and set the cup on the small table next to her, careful to use a coaster so the wooden table wouldn't get stained. Laura settled into her favourite chair opposite her, and Caru was aware of her friend studying her.

"So what is going on? It took me four months of begging to get you to visit before. Now you just turn up after only a week or so?"

Caru sighed. "I don't even know where to begin. And I don't even know if I can explain." She chuckled humourlessly. "I fear if I told you everything, you would call Auntie Joan right now and have me committed."

Laura's Auntie Joan worked for a mental health charity, Caru had volunteered for the charity a few times when she was in school.

Laura frowned. "Now you're really worrying me. Are you hearing voices?"

Caru laughed again, feeling the tension break a little. "I wish it were that simple," she said. "At least there's medication for that. But this..." she really had no idea what to say. Could she really tell Laura everything? On one hand, she really didn't want her friend to think she was mentally ill.

On the other, she needed to talk to someone about it all, or she might just explode. Talking to her mum's grave the day before had helped, but it was no substitute for speaking to someone who could respond.

She picked up her cup and sipped her tea, dimly aware of Rob whooping and cheering in the lounge.

Laura shook her head. "Guess they scored then." She smiled at Caru. "You know you can tell me anything. Anything at all. How long have we been friends? How much have we gone through together? I promise I won't call Auntie Joan. No matter how crazy you sound."

Caru sighed. "Okay, well, it all started a few days ago, though to me, it feels like months ago..."

It had been at least ten minutes since Caru had finished talking, and Laura had yet to utter a word. Caru was beginning to worry.

"Laura?" she said, leaning forward in her seat. "Are you okay?"

Laura blinked a few times then focused on Caru's face.

"You were in another... reality?"

Caru shrugged. "To be honest, I really don't know. I just know that somehow I was living a different life. One in which we weren't friends, and Charlie was dead, Jess was killed, and you were single, with no kids. No Rob."

She could see Laura was struggling to comprehend everything she had just been told, and she didn't blame her. She had lived it, and it was still difficult for her to believe.

"But you came back," Laura said, still looking a little dazed.

"Yes," Caru said. "I wish I could say I came back for you, or Charlie, or Jess, but in truth, it just happened."

She thought back to that bus ride to work and how she had wished that Jess was still alive. Maybe she had chosen to come back after all? But she hadn't realised what she was doing.

If she'd had any idea she would be returning, she would have made sure to have worked out a way to find Peter.

Laura looked at her, concern written all over her face. "Are you planning to leave again? To go back? To Peter?"

Caru shook her head. "I don't know if that's even possible, I don't know how it happened in the first place." She frowned. "So you believe me? You don't think I'm mad?"

Laura shook her head and Caru's hope was dashed.

"I don't think you're mad, in fact..." Laura got up then, and left the room without another word, and Caru frowned. She picked up her cup and Laura's and headed to the kitchen to put the kettle back on. It was getting late in the afternoon, and they would need to make dinner for the kids soon.

"Here," Laura said, coming into the kitchen. She was holding out a notebook to Caru.

Caru set the kettle down and took the notebook. She glanced down at the pages and saw Laura's neat script all over it. She scanned a few lines and gasped.

She looked up at her friend.

"You dreamed it too?"

Laura nodded. "I think I did."

Caru shook her head and continued reading. Her friend had written down the other reality in detail, including their phone conversation.

"But how?" Caru muttered. Jess hadn't mentioned any dreams. But maybe she had dismissed them. Perhaps she should ask her.

"Did you say you recorded Charlie's song?" Laura asked.

"Yeah, I did." Caru handed the notebook back to her friend and went to the hallway where she'd left her rucksack. She retrieved her phone and scrolled through the photo gallery until she found the video.

She pressed play and handed it to Laura, who watched silently, tears beginning to fall.

Charlie's voice filled the kitchen, and Caru closed her eyes. She hadn't seen him again since he'd sung to her, and then carried her to the gallery. She needed to talk to him, to thank him.

"That's so beautiful," Laura said, wiping her face with her sleeve. "His voice is amazing. He should have his own album."

Caru took her phone back and looked down at the screen at his face. Maybe that was how she could thank him. She opened her YouTube app and tapped on the upload video button. She selected the video of Charlie and tapped in a short heading and a description of Charlie and his music. Then she set her phone down, leaving the video to upload while she helped her friend to prepare dinner.

"I'm glad you believe me," she said softly to her best friend as they stood side by side, preparing vegetables.

"Always," Laura said, leaning her head on Caru's shoulder. "I'm just sorry that you lost your guy and your babies." Her voice cracked. "How can we find him again?"

Caru sighed. "I have no idea. Peter wasn't on social media. I don't remember his number. And his family came to us at Christmas, we didn't visit them, so I don't know where they live. I looked up his flat, searched for his name, and his sister's, but nothing came up. He doesn't live there. Maybe he only did because we were together." She shrugged, trying to ward off yet more tears. She felt wrung out, exhausted.

"Considering you visited another reality for several months and then came back, I would say anything is possible though, right?" Laura's voice was more hopeful than Caru could allow herself to be.

Caru turned and kissed her friend on the top of her head. "Absolutely." She didn't believe it, but hoped with every part of her being that her friend was right.

CHAPTER TWENTY

"WHAT are you doing?"

Caru looked up from where she crouched on the floor, stuffing old magazines into a bag, at Jess, who was watching her with a mixture of amusement and concern.

She shrugged. "Finally tired of the mess, I guess. I want to declutter and get some order."

Jess surveyed the room, which currently looked even more of a disaster than usual and raised an eyebrow. "Order, huh? Well, I'm about to order takeout, want some?"

Caru smiled. "Yes, please. I can't even begin to think of something to cook. No onions, though, they're still making me feel queasy." As soon as the words left her mouth she realised her mistake.

"Still? You love onions, you had them on the pizza last week. Since when do they make you feel ill?"

Caru shook her head. "It's nothing, really, think I just felt iffy the other day after my cheese and onion sandwich."

"Okay, well, how about Japanese?"

"Sounds great," Caru said, continuing to fill the bag with magazines. "Let me know what I owe you."

Jess waved her hand and left the room to go and order.

Caru sat back on her heels and sighed. When she'd got back from spending a couple of nights at Laura's, she had decided to get her room sorted in the hope it might help her sort the rest of her life. But it was harder to sort than she could have ever imagined. It had been different in her other life, when there just wasn't any stuff to worry about. But when she tried to pack things away, or sort things to donate to charity, she remembered why she had kept the item, remembered the significance of it, or felt that she might still use it. Or in the case of her many unfinished projects, that she might one day finish it. She hadn't needed an excess of stuff in her other life, but in this one, it seemed she still had some gaps she needed to fill.

She thought back to the last time she'd sat in her kitchen, and said goodbye to Peter for the day. She remembered the feeling of wholeness she'd had, and wondered where it had come from. Why did she have the feeling in that life and not in this one?

Her gaze moved to her desk where she kept her paperwork.

The letters.

Though she knew now they hadn't really been written by her father, her younger self hadn't known that. Her younger self in the other reality had believed that her father loved her. That he believed in her, that he was proud of her.

Tears filled her eyes and she mourned the loss of those letters. She had read them several times, and had planned to read them to her own children, so that they'd know that they were loved and wanted.

Maybe she still could.

She jumped up from her crouched position on the floor and dug through her desk drawer until she found a stationery set she'd bought years ago and never used. She pushed aside all the clutter on her desk and sat on top of the clothing pile on her desk chair. She got out her favourite pen, and began to recreate the letters from her dad. She couldn't remember them word for word, but she could remember how they'd made her feel, and that was more important.

When she'd written a few letters, her stomach growled. She stood up and stretched, and picked up her cold cup of tea. She drank it and surveyed the room. She had hoped that writing the words of love and encouragement would help to fill the gaps, but she still felt too attached to her possessions.

She wondered if she was going about it all wrong. Marie Kondo always said to sort clothes first, because there was less attachment to them. But having just got her colourful wardrobe back, Caru wasn't inclined to part with it again. Even if she did have items that she hadn't worn for years, and things that didn't go with anything else. She sighed. Perhaps the KonMari method just didn't work for reality shifters like herself.

She chuckled to herself. Reality shifter. It sounded like something out of a sci-fi movie. But then, how else could she explain it?

She was looking forward to seeing Charlie the next day. She had taken the rest of the week off, as promised to Kevin, but she wanted to get back to work. Having written the letters, she now had an idea for a whole new range of cards to print, which she would make next weekend. She couldn't wait to get inky again.

She slugged down the rest of the cold tea and got her things ready for the next day. She was just putting some of the magazines that she'd decided to part with into a plastic bag when she heard Jess calling her.

"Is it here? I didn't hear the buzzer?" she asked as she entered the kitchen. Jess waved her over to the sofa, and as Caru approached, she heard a familiar sound coming from Jess' phone.

She frowned. "What are you watching?" She sat next to Jess and was surprised to see her watching the video she'd taken of Charlie. She was going to ask how Jess had got hold of it, when she remembered suddenly that she had uploaded it to YouTube while she was at Laura's earlier in the week.

"My friend sent me this, isn't he amazing?"

"Jess, that's my video."

Jess looked up from the screen at Caru, her eyes wide. "Seriously?"

"Yeah, he's the busker I told you about."

Jess looked back at the screen. Charlie finished the song and looked up at the camera. Caru heard her own voice say "That was beautiful." And Charlie's reply - "It wasn't a dream, was it?"

Tears filled Caru's eyes. She still hadn't had a chance to tell him properly what had really happened.

"What did he mean, it wasn't a dream?" Jess asked,

scrolling up.

Caru was trying to think of how to answer when she noticed the number of views under the video and couldn't help herself from grabbing Jess' phone out of her hands.

"Are you serious?" she gasped.

"What?" Jess asked, trying to see the screen.

"The video has had fifty thousand views!" Caru breathed. She scrolled down to the comments and saw people's reactions to the video. Some were saying how beautiful it was, and some, just a couple, said that they'd experienced some weird dreams recently too.

'Had it affected everyone?' Caru wondered.

"That's amazing," Jess said, taking her phone back. "Maybe he'll get a deal or something out of it."

"That really would be amazing," Caru said, wishing she had a phone number for Charlie so she could call him and let him know.

"He looks familiar, you know." Jess said thoughtfully. "I feel like I know him from somewhere."

A flash of memory from a dream in another life came to mind, and Caru saw Jess sitting next to Charlie on the step, saying he would look after her now. It was gone in a flash and she looked at Jess. "You probably just walked past him in town or something," she said, brushing it off, afraid to find out if Jess remembered anything.

Jess shrugged. "Yeah, probably. I think I've probably seen him busking in town a couple of times."

The buzzer went then and Caru sighed in relief. Saved by the bell.

Despite feeling afraid to find out if Jess had any knowledge of the other reality, once they were sat at the kitchen bar, the boxes of Japanese food open between them and a bottle of wine opened, Caru couldn't help but ask.

"Have you had any weird dreams lately?" she asked, taking a big bite of her food, which was still a bit too hot to eat quickly.

"Dreams?" Jess frowned. "I don't normally remember them, to be honest. I had a few odd ones last week, but I couldn't tell you why they were odd now." She picked up her chopstick. "Why?"

Caru shook her head. "Oh, no reason, I was just thinking about Charlie's dream."

"The one he wrote the song about? Why did he think it was real, do you think?"

Caru quickly put some noodles in her mouth. "No idea," she mumbled through her mouthful.

"Shall we take this to the sofa?" Jess asked. "We haven't had a movie marathon in ages."

Caru swallowed her mouthful and smiled. "Sounds like a plan." They moved everything to the coffee table, and as the opening music started up, Caru tried to let go of the many thoughts swirling around in her mind, but she couldn't help but remember sitting in that very spot, with Peter, as they watched a movie. She missed his scent, his voice, his arms, his lips, and of course, his cooking. She ate more noodles and pushed down the wave of emotion threatening to spill from her eyes.

She wondered if she would ever get over him. But how could she spend her life grieving the loss of someone she'd never even met? Perhaps if she could convince herself it had all just been a dream, it would make it easier to bear.

Caru was impatient to get to work the next morning, yet she still managed to end up having to run to catch the bus. It was because she still hadn't managed to sort and wash her clothes, and it had taken her ages to find an outfit she wanted to wear.

She had also been distracted by reading through all the comments on the video of Charlie. It now had four hundred thousand views and she couldn't wait to tell him. She just hoped that he wouldn't mind her posting it without his permission.

She looked out the window, feeling sweaty and a little out of breath. She needed a new plan. Decluttering her room was just one step, she needed to take charge of her finances and her work situation, and sort her life out. She felt she had learned enough from her other life to make a real difference, and if she kept reading and repeating the words of love and encouragement, maybe she would begin to feel as she did in her other life. Even though she didn't have savings, she knew she could start saving now. It might be a while before she could save up enough for a home, but she might be able to at least save enough to go travelling. It would be amazing to go to all the places she'd written about.

After what felt like an eternity, the bus came to a groaning halt at her usual stop in town, and Caru hurried up the high street to the coffee shop.

As she neared, she could see a crowd gathered, and she frowned. There seemed to be too many people to be queuing for a coffee.

She got a bit closer and could hear the familiar sound of Charlie's voice. She stopped in her tracks when she realised that the crowd of people were huddled around his step, watching him play. Some of them were filming him, others had their eyes closed, listening intently.

He was singing her song.

Tears came to her eyes as she listened to him singing about the cup of tea she brought him every morning.

He sang the last few words and opened his eyes. The crowd burst into applause, and someone handed him a cup of tea. He smiled and thanked them, and took a sip. Some of the crowd stayed to watch him sing the next song, and some moved on, off to work or to do their shopping.

Caru moved closer, and before he lost himself in the music, Charlie spotted her and smiled. She waved her hand at the coffee shop and he nodded.

She went inside to get a coffee, feeling sad that she didn't need to buy him a tea, but elated that he seemed to be getting the appreciation and recognition he deserved. She came outside again, holding her hot cup, and waited until Charlie finished his next song.

The crowd clapped and cheered again and threw a few coins into his guitar case.

"You'll be able to buy your own tea soon," Caru teased in the moment of quiet after the applause.

Charlie looked up at her and grinned. "I don't know what's going on this morning, but I like it," he said.

"I think I do," Caru said. "And I'm hoping you'll still like it when I tell you what I did."

Charlie frowned and sipped his tea while Caru pulled out her phone, opened the YouTube app and showed him the screen.

"I uploaded it last week," she said softly. "It seems a few people thought it was worth sharing and it's gone viral."

Charlie looked at the number of views, his eyes wide. "Wow, that's crazy."

Caru winced. "I should have asked you, but I thought it would be okay, that a few people would like it and that would be it."

"Of course it's okay. It's a good video, I'm glad you shared it." He handed her phone back to her. "But I am still waiting."

"Waiting?" Caru shook her head. "Oh, of course, I'm sorry. Thank you, Charlie, for looking after me the other week. I'm sorry I passed out at your feet. I appreciate you taking me to the gallery."

Charlie chuckled. "You're welcome, but that's not what I meant." He tilted his head. "I meant I'm still waiting for the answer to my question. It was real, wasn't it?"

Caru sighed. "Oh, that."

"I still remember every detail, clear as day. I never remember dreams that clearly, never."

Caru looked at her phone, she only had two minutes to get to the gallery before ten, and she didn't want to be late on her first day back.

"Can you meet me later?" she asked. "You could come back to mine for dinner?"

Charlie nodded. "Sure, shall I come to the gallery at four?"

Caru smiled. "That's perfect." She held the lid tightly on her coffee cup then turned toward the gallery.

"I'll see you later," Charlie called after her.

CHAPTER TWENTY ONE

"ARE you really not going to speak until we get back to your house?" Charlie asked, a smile tugging at the corner of his mouth.

Caru smiled back. "I'm sorry," she said, looking around the half empty bus. "I guess I don't really know where to start, so it feels weird discussing it in public."

"Fair enough. I can be patient a little longer."

Caru shook her head. "I'm sorry I didn't come to thank you sooner, I had to go visit my friend, and sort my room, and... figure things out." Her voice trailed off, and she looked away, out the window into the coming twilight.

"It's okay, I could sense that you were... in shock. That things shifted for you, that morning last week, when I sang to you."

Caru's eyes filled with tears, and she continued to stare out the window, but nodded her head in confirmation.

She felt Charlie touch her hand, and she looked down

and smiled through her tears. It was the first time they had touched, and it was comforting. She turned her hand upward and interlocked her hand with his. She looked at him, and saw his surprise. She searched his face, looking for the connection they'd had in her dreams.

Was this the real reason she had returned? Was she meant to be with Charlie? The thought of it made her feel disloyal to Peter, but she didn't let go of Charlie's hand.

The bus lurched to a sudden stop, and Caru looked up to see they were at her usual stop. Thank goodness the bus driver knew her so well, otherwise they would have had a long walk down dark lanes to get back to the house.

She got up and pulled Charlie up with her, and he picked up his guitar as they made their way off the bus, hands still intertwined.

"Thank you," she called to the driver over her shoulder.

"Always happy to help," the driver replied.

She and Charlie walked down the lane to her home, the silence still heavy between them. She wondered what was going through Charlie's mind, and then figured she might not want to know.

When they approached the front door, the security lights came on, but before Caru could put her key in the lock, the door opened, and Mark came out holding a bag of recycling.

"Oh hey, Caru, good day?"

Caru smiled at her neighbour and nodded. She saw him glance down at her hand in Charlie's and his eyebrows raise.

"This is Charlie," she said. "Charlie, this is Mark."

The two of them nodded to each other, both looking a little confused. Caru stepped into the foyer, with Charlie behind her.

"He seems nice," Charlie said.

Caru remembered Mark in the other reality, trying to help Jess, and the kindness he'd shown her. She gulped in a breath and nodded. "Uh huh," she replied, not trusting herself not to cry.

They reached the door to her flat, both a little out of breath, but still holding hands. Caru opened the door and headed straight for the kitchen. She still hadn't got her room into an acceptable state, so there was no way she would let Charlie see it.

She let go of his hand to fill the kettle, and he shrugged his guitar off his shoulder then set it down on the floor.

"Tea?" she asked with a smile as the kettle began to boil.

He smiled back. "Of course."

Caru pulled two bags out of the canister and frowned. "You know, I just realised, I never actually ever asked you if you liked tea. I just started buying it for you, and assumed that because you took it, you liked it. But maybe you were just cold? Or too polite?"

Charlie chuckled, and Caru realised that she had never heard him laugh before. It was a beautiful sound.

"I am rather partial to hot chocolate, but tea is a close second."

Caru smiled at him. "Oh, well, in that case, screw the tea." She chucked the two bags back in the canister and opened her cupboard and pulled out the special hot chocolate she had bought months ago and never got round to drinking.

"Now that's more like it," Charlie said, still chuckling. "Do I hear the kettle?"

Caru looked up to see Jess standing in the doorway, her eyes on Charlie.

"Hi, you're Charlie," she said. "I'm Jess." She held her hand out, and Charlie shook it, looking a little bewildered.

"I know you," he said.

Jess laughed, her hand still clasped in his. "That's exactly what I said when I watched your video. I felt like I knew you somehow, but I wasn't exactly sure how."

Charlie pulled his gaze from Jess' face to look at Caru.

She sighed and nodded her head in confirmation to his thoughts. That Jess was the dark haired girl he'd mentioned from his dream.

He looked back at Jess and smiled, finally letting go of her hand. "Well, however we know each other, it's nice to meet you properly, Jess."

"Likewise," Jess replied. "That song really is incredible. Have you seen the views? It's up to a million now."

"A million?" Caru said. "That's amazing!" She pulled her phone out to check, and sure enough, the video had just over one million views.

Caru grinned at Charlie. "You'll be famous!"

Charlie blushed and accepted the cup of hot chocolate she offered him. "Oh I doubt it, I'm sure there are cat videos out there that have had tens of millions of views."

Jess laughed and made herself a cup of tea and started heading back to her room.

"I'm making dinner," Caru called after her. "Want some?"

"Please!" Jess called back.

Caru picked up her hot chocolate and motioned for Charlie to follow her to the living room space. They sat down on opposite ends of the same sofa, and silently sipped their drinks for a few minutes. Caru still wasn't sure how to begin, but now that Charlie had recognised Jess, it wasn't as though denying everything that had happened was an option anymore.

"It wasn't a dream," she said, meeting his eye. "But then I think you knew that already."

"I did, but I couldn't figure out how?"

Caru sighed. "I still have no idea how, but I do know that one day, I somehow ended up in a very different reality, and then four months later, I ended up back here, the day after I left." She shrugged. "Did I reality shift? Time travel? Hallucinate? I have no idea. But the fact that it affected everyone I know, not just me, makes me think that it was something bigger. Even some of the people commenting on your video said they'd had weird dreams."

Charlie was quiet for a while. "But why? What was the purpose? Do you know?"

Caru shook her head. "I don't know. At first, I just thought it was a world where all my dreams had come true. And to be honest, many of them did. But it was a world where I didn't buy cups of tea for strangers, I didn't spend my time making gifts for friends, and being creative, and people I loved weren't there. Instead, I was confident, focused, and had actually prioritised my own goals, my own needs." She blushed a little at the thought of Peter fulfilling her needs.

"Peter," Charlie said, reading her expression. "You kept saying Peter when you came round after passing out."

"He was my fiancé," Caru said. "But we hadn't had time to tell anyone yet, the ring was too small, and it was being resized. I was meant to collect it the day you sang to me."

"But it wouldn't be there to collect now," Charlie mused. "Can you find him? Do you know where he lives?"

Caru shook her head. "I've tried everything, but I don't have any contact details for him, and all my searches turned up nothing. We met in Peru, and our meeting shaped our paths from that point. When he didn't meet me, he probably met some other woman, and is now going to marry her and have babies with her in their beautiful house."

Caru knew she sounded bitter and resentful, but it was difficult not to. The thought of Peter being with another woman was like a knife to her chest.

She looked at Charlie. "Maybe if I knew the purpose of all this, it would be easier to bear, but at the moment, it just feels like some bizarre glitch in the matrix that was created to torture me by giving me everything I ever wanted, only to rip it away again."

"Was the other world really so perfect?" Charlie asked softly. He drank the rest of his hot chocolate and set the mug down on the windowsill.

Caru noticed he had chocolate foam around his mouth and she leaned forward to wipe it away, without stopping to wonder if it was appropriate.

"No," she said softly, her hand still resting on his stubbly cheek. "Because you weren't in it anymore."

Charlie leaned forward, and Caru instinctively leaned towards him, but before their lips could meet, she heard Jess coming back into the kitchen.

"I actually have a real strong craving for-"

Caru pulled away from Charlie as Jess clocked their positions and stopped talking.

"Um, sorry," she averted her gaze to the ceiling and

waved her phone with the food delivery app open. "I was just thinking I really want a curry tonight. Shall we order instead?"

Caru looked at Charlie and he shrugged his assent.

"Sure," Caru said, picking up their empty mugs and making her way to the kitchen counter. "Let's order in."

"Are you sure this is okay?"

Caru tucked the sheet into the corners of the sofa, and shook out the blanket.

"Of course. There are no busses this late, and it's too cold out there to walk far." She looked down at the makeshift bed. "We do have a spare room, but it's full to the brim with my stuff, otherwise you could have stayed in there."

"This is amazing," Charlie said, sitting down on the clean sheet. "Thank you. For dinner. For helping me not feel like I'm crazy. For caring. This is going way beyond a cup of tea."

Caru chuckled. "I guess. Where do you live, anyway? Near town?" She remembered Jess' comments about fancying a homeless person.

"I live with my dad on the estate at the edge of town. It's a shit hole thanks to his love of booze, but it's a roof over the head."

"Oh," Caru said, relieved that he had a home, but sad that it wasn't a good one.

"You thought I was homeless?" Charlie asked, unbuttoning his jeans and slipping them off.

Caru averted her gaze and shook her head. "No, I just

wondered. I realise I don't know anything about you. I never even knew your name until..."

"Until I died?"

Caru looked up to see him standing closer to her. She looked into his eyes and nodded.

He reached out to touch her cheek, and she closed her eyes. She could sense him leaning closer, and just as his lips were about to meet hers, her heart thumped and Peter's face came into her mind.

She pulled back a little and opened her eyes.

"I'm sorry," she whispered. "I can't."

Charlie nodded, looking more contrite than frustrated.

"I understand," he replied. "I'm sorry."

She reached out and put her hand on his chest. She could feel his heart beating steadily though his thin t-shirt.

"Don't be," she said.

Before she could change her mind, Caru left the lounge, and in the bathroom, set out a new toothbrush and a clean towel for Charlie to use. Then she quickly brushed her teeth and her hair, then headed to her still cluttered room.

It wasn't until she was in bed, with the lights off, that she finally allowed herself to think of Peter. To think of the last time she had seen him, as he finished his breakfast and flew out the door, a trail of cornflakes in his wake.

She wondered where he was in the world and if she would ever see him again. The tears flowed steadily, and she grieved for the loss of such a beautiful man.

Her thoughts turned to Charlie, and she wondered if what she felt for him really was attraction, or something sweeter, purer, and non-sexual.

Unable to work it out, she drifted into a dreamless sleep.

CHAPTER TWENTY TWO

CARU stared at the words on her laptop screen, not quite comprehending their meaning. Despite having read the email three times, it still hadn't quite sunk in.

A record company had seen Charlie singing (the video was now at 2.3 million views and constantly increasing) and they were interested in talking to him.

They wanted to record *Faith in a Teacup*. And they wanted to make an album with him.

Caru read the email a fourth time and cursed Charlie's lack of mobile phone again. It was late on Friday night, so she would have to wait two whole days until she could find him on Monday morning on his usual step and give him the news.

This was huge.

Caru couldn't stop smiling. Her heart had felt heavy since she had returned, and despite being so glad to be among her best friends again, the grief for her dream life had been suffocating.

But this news had lifted something. Made it worth it somehow. She had no doubt that this would change Charlie's life. He could move out of his dad's place, get his own home, and be paid properly for his music.

Maybe even find a woman to be with.

She touched her cheek, remembering his hand there, his body close to hers as they got so close to kissing, twice.

She wondered, for the millionth time in the last four days, if she had made the right decision when she had pulled away. She had seen Charlie at his usual spot every day, and she had bought him a cup of hot chocolate just that morning, and they had exchanged their usual pleasantries as if nothing had ever happened.

Caru sighed and closed her laptop. She would reply to the email tomorrow and tell them she would give the information to him on Monday.

She should have asked Charlie where he lived, then she could have visited him the next day. Well, there was no point dwelling on the 'if only's, she needed to continue clearing her room out over the weekend, so that she could print the new range of cards on Sunday. She still hadn't tried out her new ideas yet.

Caru took her dinner plate and cup out to the kitchen and rinsed them off before stacking them in the dishwasher, and she was staring at her reflection in the window when Jess came into the room, talking loudly on the phone.

"Okay, fine! I'll decide on the restaurant, just make sure you're wearing something decent?" She dumped her crockery in the sink, nodded at Caru, then giggling at the response she got on the phone, headed back out the door.

Shaking her head and feeling more like a parent than a housemate, Caru rinsed off Jess' plate and cutlery and stacked them neatly in the dishwasher. She could hear Jess giggling again, and she prayed silently that whoever she was setting up a date with was a good one, and wasn't called Henry.

She headed back to her room, wondering how much of the other reality (Timeline? World?) might end up filtering into this one. Obviously she wouldn't be buying a house, or moving out, so Jess wouldn't have Henry move in, but he might still appear? And there might be other people who could appear. Like Becky, or maybe even...

Despite her promise to herself that she would get an early night, Caru found herself on her phone, doing search after search with all of the information she had on Peter.

But by two in the morning, she had to admit defeat and finally turn out the light.

Caru was in the middle of a sneezing fit, brought on by trying to clean underneath her desk, when she heard the front door close and voices in the hallway.

She blew her nose and wondered if Jess had brought her date home. She never normally did that, but maybe Pyre had finally delivered?

Tired from cleaning and sorting all day (not that you could really tell from the piles of stuff still cluttering her room) Caru gave into her curiosity and went out to the kitchen to see who Jess was talking to.

"Caru! You're still up! Or did we wake you?"

Caru smiled at Jess who stumbled slightly in her high heels. Then she looked at the guy and her eyes widened.

"Charlie! Hi, um, wow, I didn't realise you were on Pyre..."

Charlie chuckled, and Jess giggled as she filled the kettle, splashing water all over the counter.

"No, no, he doesn't even have a phone," Jess said. "He rescued me."

Caru gave Charlie a puzzled look and took over the tea making in case Jess burned herself.

"That's overstating it a bit. I happened to be in the same bar as Jess and her, um, date," Charlie said, settling onto a stool at the counter. "It seemed like he was getting a little too familiar, so I stopped to say hi and Jess pretty much begged me to get her away from him." He shrugged and grinned at Jess, who was trying to take off her shoes without falling over. "How could I resist?"

Caru said nothing, and was waiting for her body to react, to feel the flush of jealousy rise up, but in truth, she felt nothing.

She watched Charlie reach out to assist Jess in removing her shoes, and as her housemate held onto his arm a bit longer than necessary, oddly, it felt... right. And not odd at all.

She smiled at Charlie. "Thank you. For looking out for Jess, for bringing her home."

Charlie tilted his head a little at her tone, but said nothing. She hoped he could tell that she was genuinely grateful. Not just because he saved had her friend, but because she finally knew that it was not meant to be between them. That maybe, he was destined for someone else, and that maybe she was too.

"Jess?" she said, pouring the hot water into Jess' favourite mug and taking it over to the sofa where her housemate was now sprawled. There were gentle sighs coming from underneath her mess of dark curls, and Caru smiled.

"Is she?" Charlie asked, sipping his tea.

Caru chuckled softly. "Yeah, she's out." Caru set the tea on the coffee table nearby, but not close enough to be knocked over, grabbed the blanket from the other sofa, and draped it over her friend. She was going to have one hell of a hangover in the morning.

"Do you want to stay too?" Caru asked Charlie, joining him at the counter. She glanced at the clock, it was gone midnight.

"Twice in one week? What will the neighbours think?" Charlie teased.

Caru laughed softly. "That Jess is having a great time."

"Jess?" Charlie said, so much meant by his simple question.

Caru smiled. "I know that there is... something between us. A connection. But it's not because we are meant to be together. I think it was because we needed to help each other."

Charlie frowned. "How am I helping you?"

"By helping my friend. Taking care of her. Being there for her."

"That's not helping you directly though, you've helped me so much with buying me tea, inspiring a song, all those views on YouTube."

"Oh!" Caru said, sloshing some of the tea out of her cup onto the counter as she remembered the news she had for Charlie. "Wait here!"

She jumped up and ran to her room, and grabbed the printout of the email she had received the night before. She couldn't believe she had forgotten about it already.

She came back into the kitchen and sat down next to Charlie again. She handed him the paper, and he scanned it, his eyes getting wider until he reached the end and his mouth dropped open in shock.

"Is this real?" he asked.

Caru nodded. "It came through last night. I wanted to tell you straight away, but of course you don't have a phone. I thought I was going to have to wait until Monday morning to tell you."

Charlie read the email twice more, while Caru finished her tea.

"I think I'd better get a phone," Charlie said, with awe in his voice.

"Oh, actually, I have an old one you're welcome to have. It's not great, the battery doesn't last as long as it should but the screen isn't cracked, and I have the charger for it."

Charlie looked up at her, and smiled. "What did I do to deserve you? You're my angel."

Caru laughed, feeling a bit embarrassed. "Sorry, it's my superhero complex coming out. If I think I can help someone, then I will, regardless of whether it's appropriate or not." Except when she was in alternate realities, apparently, where she focused on looking after herself.

"Well don't ever change. Because without you, none of this would have been possible."

Caru grinned. "Someone would have recognised your genius eventually," she said. "I'm sure of it."

Charlie laughed. "Maybe. Maybe not." He yawned.

"Why don't you take Jess's bed? She won't be going anywhere tonight."

"Do you think she'll mind?"

Caru shook her head. "Nah, you're her knight in shining armour. You deserve the bed this time."

Caru picked up the empty cups and rinsed them out before putting them in the dishwasher. "Your toothbrush is still in the bathroom, I'll put a clean towel out."

Charlie stood up and reached out to pull Caru into a hug. She was surprised, but not unwilling, and allowed him to wrap his arms around her and squeeze her tight.

"If there's anything I can do for you," he whispered. "Just let me know."

Caru breathed in his scent and nodded into his chest. "I will."

She pulled back, and wished that she had at least let him kiss her just once, but she knew now that he was not hers to kiss.

"Good night, Charlie," she said. "I'll sort the phone out in the morning, so you can call the record company first thing on Monday."

"Thank you, Caru. Goodnight."

CHAPTER TWENTY THREE

THE next morning, Caru went into the kitchen and saw that the blanket she had covered Jess with was on the floor. She hoped that Jess hadn't freaked out when she found Charlie in her bed. But clearly they had spent at least some of the night together in her room.

Caru sighed and picked up the blanket and folded it, placing it neatly back on the sofa. Though she was happy for them, there was a tiny part of her that was envious. Even though she knew that she and Charlie were just meant to be friends.

She poured some cereal and put the kettle on, then sat at the counter to eat. She'd had enough of cleaning and sorting, she planned to get some printing done, and maybe try to finish a sewing project she had begun months ago. As much as she wanted to bring some of the stillness from her other life into this one, she was finding it difficult to relax, to sit still, to just be. There were so many projects she wanted to do, and the idea of being bored scared her. Because boredom meant thinking, and when she thought too much, she got overwhelmed with sadness. She decided to read her letters again, and turn the phrases into cards. Perhaps printing the words would help to imprint them on her soul, and help her to believe them.

"Morning."

Caru looked up to see Jess stood in the doorway, looking hungover and sheepish, her dark hair sticking out in all directions.

Caru smiled at her housemate. "Morning. Sleep well?"

Jess blushed and looked down at her penguin slippers. "Yeah, I think so." She rubbed her head. "Drank too much last night."

Caru chuckled and got up to re-boil the kettle. "Maybe just a bit. Sit down. I'll make you a coffee."

Jess followed her instructions and sat on the other stool. "So you're not mad?"

Caru turned to look at her. "Mad? What for? Actually, I think you and Charlie are just right for each other."

Jess looked surprised. "Really? But I thought you two liked each other? You looked really close the other night."

Caru filled the mug with hot water and stirred the milk and coffee in. "Yeah, at first I thought maybe there might have been a spark, but there wasn't." She set the mug in front of her housemate. "If you like him, go for it. He really is a very decent guy."

Jess grinned. "He does seem lovely, I mean, we didn't do anything last night, I woke up on the sofa and went to bed, and we just cuddled." She shrugged. "I don't think any other guy would have just been happy to hold me like that without trying to take it further."

Caru sat back down to finish her breakfast. Before she could respond, Charlie came into the kitchen, barefoot, wearing just his jeans and t-shirt.

"Morning," he said. "May I have a shower?"

"Of course," Caru replied. "Just grab a bigger towel from the cupboard in the hallway."

He smiled and went out to the cupboard. Caru heard it open and close, then the bathroom door close and the shower start up.

"Are you sure you're okay with this?" Jess asked.

Caru looked her in the eye. "Absolutely. I get the feeling that things are going to take off for Charlie very soon, and I can't think of anyone better to share it with him than you."

Jess reached out to hug her and Caru squeezed her back. "Love you."

Caru smiled. "Love you too."

"Caru, these are fabulous," Kevin said, looking through the new cards she had printed on the weekend.

"Thanks, I had fun with these ones, once I got started, I couldn't stop."

Kevin counted them all off against the invoice and then took them over to the card rack and started putting them out on display. "I think these will sell really well. Everyone loves to be told they are loved! Have you thought about selling them online? Or at fairs? Because you should."

Caru nodded. "Actually I was thinking just that on the weekend. If I printed solidly for a few days, I'd have enough stock to start an online shop. I've got quite a few followers on Instagram, I might start posting them on there too. I do need to make some money from my crafting. My bank account is looking a bit sad again."

"What about wedding invitations? They're big business, and you can charge a better price point than greeting cards."

Caru's gaze drifted to the cupboard under the counter, where the custom thank you cards she had made were now collecting dust.

"It's a possibility," she said. "I got put off of making custom cards after those thank you cards were never collected."

"Oh!" Kevin said. "Didn't I tell you? The woman came to get them while you were off for the week. She said there had been a death in the family, and was really apologetic for the delay in collecting them. She paid twenty percent more than your quote to make up for it."

Caru's eyes widened. "Really? That's great! I thought I was going to have to just burn them."

"I was going to add the money to your usual pay, but you could have it now if you need it?"

"No, add it to my pay, that's brilliant." Caru was thrilled. She got her notebook and pen out. "Maybe I should consider more custom orders, though I think selling wholesale to independent shops could work well too."

Kevin finished arranging the cards and sat down behind the counter. "You'd better get printing then! In the meantime, shall we get a head start on sorting the Spring Exhibition?"

Kevin pulled out the gallery diary and grabbed a pen.

"Okay, first thing to decide, which artists will we feature?"

Caru peered through the window into the empty, dark space, and in her mind's eye, could see how it looked in the other reality. With her desk opposite Becky's, and colourful posters adorning the walls of all the tours they booked, and the holiday destinations they covered. She looked up at the 'To Let' sign, and decided on a whim to call the agent and see how much it cost to rent. She assumed that it would be what she was paying in the other reality, in which case, it would be way out of her range, but perhaps it was less? Perhaps she could rent it and start her own shop?

She took out her phone and tapped in the number, and waited for someone to answer.

"Oh, hello, I was just wondering how much the property on St John's Street was to rent."

She waited for the agent to look up the details and respond.

"Oh, that's cheaper than I imagined," she said, her heart beating a little faster. "Do you have any interest in it? I don't think I'm ready just yet, but it would be the perfect spot."

The agent assured her that it had been empty for ten months, (which was how long she had been renting it in the other reality) which is why it was now cheaper. They didn't expect it to be rented out before Christmas.

"Okay, thank you, I will get back to you."

The agent hung up and she stared in to the darkness beyond the window for a while longer before setting off back to the high street to catch the bus home. It was starting to get dark already, and she shivered inside her coat. It seemed like she needed to start wearing more layers.

On the bus ride home, Caru pulled out her notebook and started doodling possible ideas for her new business. She could sell local crafts as well as her printing, and maybe run workshops and weekly classes. There would need to be several income streams to ensure she could cover rent and bills, and hiring help when needed. She would need to work out how much she would need to save up and how long it might take.

Would it be possible to open by Christmas? It would be a lot to do in less than two months.

Lost in thought, Caru hadn't realised that they'd reached her stop until the bus stopped and the bell rang. She shoved her notebook and pen in her bag and ran down to the front. She stepped off and said thank you over her shoulder.

"Anything is possible!" the driver called back.

Before she could turn around to question his odd words, the doors closed and he pulled away from the curb.

Was it the bus driver? Was he the one causing the weird shifts in reality?

She stood on the pavement for a moment as she thought back to when her reality had shifted the first time, then back again. It always seemed to happen when she was on the bus. And his odd words... she thought back to the many odd things that had been said.

"Anything is possible," she muttered to herself as she walked down the lane to her home.

A magical bus driver, whatever next?

She chuckled to herself as she headed to the front door, and stopped when the security lights flicked on and she saw a figure sat on the doorstep.

"Charlie! What are you doing here? Jess is working late tonight."

He stood up slowly, looking stiff from having been sat on the stone for too long.

Caru saw the bag at his feet next to his guitar. "Everything okay?"

He shook his head and Caru saw the strain in his expression. She opened the front door and ushered him in, grabbing the post from the basket as they made their way upstairs.

It was only once they were safely in the flat, and Charlie had a hot chocolate in front of him, that he finally spoke.

"My dad's thrown me out," he said, the pain obvious in his eyes. "The last few days he's been drinking more than usual, and was getting a bit... irate."

Caru peered more closely at Charlie and saw that he had bruises down the side of his face. Her heart ached.

"Well you'll stay here. And you won't have to sleep on the sofa, I think it's time I finally cleared out the junk room. There's a mattress in there under all the junk, I'm sure we could pick up a second-hand bed frame."

Charlie looked up at her, his eyes red and full of unshed tears. "Are you sure?"

"Absolutely. Jess will agree. And our landlord is fine with us having guests. We just haven't because of using it as a junk room." She sipped her drink. "You should have called, I could have given you my key so you weren't stuck out in the cold."

Charlie pulled the phone she had given him out of his

pocket. "The battery was dead, and I didn't have time to charge it."

Caru took it from him and plugged it into the spare charger on the counter. "Sorry, I did warn you the battery was a bit crap." She sat next to him. "Did you hear back from the record label yet?"

Charlie's face lit up and he nodded. "We're meeting next week. They're going to pay for my travel to go to London to meet them."

Caru grinned. "That's brilliant! I'm so pleased for you."

"Yeah I still can't quite believe it. Have you seen the video? It's got well over three million views now."

"That's amazing! I really had no idea that it would take off like that when I posted it." Caru sipped her tea and then got up to grab some biscuits out of the cupboard. She offered some to Charlie and he inhaled several.

"I have been meaning to call you," Charlie said after washing the biscuits down with his drink.

"Oh?"

"About Jess. I mean, about what happened last weekend. I didn't know she was going to be in that pub, and when you said to take her bed, I didn't think she would get in with me." Charlie looked down at his hands. "Jess said you were okay with it, but I just wanted to ask you, because we came close to something happening between us before that, and I would hate for you to think less of me."

"Charlie," Caru said, putting her hand on his arm. "I am completely okay with it. Nothing happened between us, and I think you and Jess are a great match. I don't think I will be ready to be in a relationship again for a while."

There was a few moments of silence.

"Peter?" Charlie asked.

Caru nodded.

"What was he like?"

Caru smiled as she thought of her other-world fiancé. "He was amazing. He was an archaeologist, and an amazing cook. He was so excited when we found out I was pregnant, he would have made a great dad."

"Oh, wow, I didn't realise you were pregnant, that's just, that's so..." Charlie's voice trailed off.

"I know," Caru said softly. "I think that's why I went into shock when I realised I wasn't dreaming. Because I realised that I no longer carried the twins. And that Peter was no longer in my life."

"You talk about Peter like he's dead, but he's not. He's out there, somewhere, and if you two are meant to be, surely your paths will cross?" Charlie said as he finished his hot chocolate.

Caru nodded. "I hope so. It's hard to imagine being with someone else now, which is so strange. Before the shift, I was happily single, and had no maternal urges or need to cohabitate. But being in our house together, with two babies on the way, it felt so natural. So right. I can't quite imagine a different future now. Although, I did enquire about renting the property on St John's Street. It was where my business was in the other reality."

Charlie got up to refill the kettle. "Are you thinking of starting a travel company?"

Caru shook her head. "No, I was thinking of a gift shop, full of local crafts and maybe running workshops. It's not a huge space, but it's big enough for a table for four people. I could teach printing or sewing or crochet. I could even get in other artists to teach other things."

"Maybe some music workshops?" Charlie asked with a grin as he leaned against the counter.

Caru grinned back. "Yeah, why not? Anything is possible." She remembered the bus driver. "You know, I'm beginning to think that it was the bus driver who did all of this."

"Excuse me?" Charlie laughed. "What do you mean?"

"The bus driver. He always says odd things to me. Things that have related to the shift from one reality to another. At least, I think it's been the same bus driver."

"An angel in disguise perhaps?" Charlie teased.

Caru laughed and accepted the tea top up. "Yeah maybe. They say they come in all guises."

"Does that mean you could ask him? The bus driver? About Peter? Maybe he would know how to find him." Charlie's tone was no longer teasing.

Caru tried to imagine asking the driver if he knew how to find her soulmate from the other reality and shook her head at herself. It seemed like such a ridiculous idea. He'd probably think she'd completely lost the plot.

And maybe she had.

"Honey! I'm hooome!"

Caru chuckled. "Jess is back. I'll leave you two to chat."

She stood up and Charlie put his hand on hers briefly. "Thank you, Caru. For everything."

"Charlie! What are you doing here?"

Caru put her cup in the sink and left her housemate to be filled in on the situation by Charlie.

She headed back to her room, determined to finish sorting out her wardrobe. In the last week she had done several loads of washing, and had picked up some extra hangers, so she could hang everything up. She stopped in the doorway, waiting for her energy saver bulb to brighten. She surveyed her room. There was definite improvement, but there was still a long way to go. At least she could actually see her desk now, and her floor. There were no longer clothes everywhere, or piles of unfinished projects. Then again, she had promised Charlie she would clear the spare room, which meant that her room would get cluttered up again with all the junk she'd been storing there.

She sighed and pulled her hair back into a bobble, then set to work on sorting and hanging her clothes. She occasionally threw an item into the bag that she planned to donate, and enjoyed sorting her clothing into colours. Her other world wardrobe had definitely been too dull.

An hour later, Jess stuck her head round the door. "Hey, we're ordering pizza, you want some?"

Caru looked up from where she was sat on her bed, folding her t-shirts KonMari style.

"I would love pizza," she said, her stomach growling. "Get me a small one if you and Charlie are sharing?"

"Sure, the usual, no onions?"

"Yeah that would be great, thanks."

Jess nodded and left the room, and Caru finished folding up the rest of her t-shirts and tucked them into the drawer. She picked up her phone and saw several messages from Laura.

She opened them and gasped. She tapped on Laura's number and waited impatiently while it rang.

"Where the hell have you been?" Laura demanded loudly.

Caru winced and pulled the phone away from her ear

and put it on speakerphone. "I'm sorry, I was busy tidying. What do you mean, you think you've found him?"

"I'm sending you the article now, there's a picture and everything. Is it him?"

Caru's phone beeped and she opened the link that Laura sent, her heart pounding in her ears. It took a few seconds to load, and she impatiently scanned the headline then scrolled down until she found the image. She tapped on it and zoomed in, and when the face became clearer, her heart thudded to a halt.

It wasn't him.

She let her breath out in a rush.

"It's not him," she whispered.

Laura sighed. "Oh shit. I'm so sorry, I honestly thought it might be. Same name, the right profession. You never described him to me but this guy looked cute."

"He does look cute," Caru agreed, scrutinising the photo. "But my Peter was gorgeous." She sighed. "Thank you for trying, but I really just don't think it's meant to be. How do you find someone who doesn't do social media? It's pretty impossible these days."

"It must be possible," Laura insisted stubbornly. "I won't stop looking."

Caru closed the article and smiled at her best friend's persistence. "Thanks, but you don't have to. I just have to get used to the idea that I won't see him again."

"Caru! Pizza!"

"Laura, my dinner is ready, but thank you again."

"Still not giving up," Laura replied. "Caru ti!"

"Caru ti," Caru echoed before hanging up. She went out to the kitchen and accepted the glass of wine Charlie offered her. Jess was still talking to the pizza delivery guy at the door.

"You okay?" he asked, noticing the look on her face.

She shook her head. "Laura thought she'd found him. Peter." She sighed. "I guess I got my hopes up for a moment."

Charlie grimaced. "That's harsh. Surely it must be possible to find him though?"

"I'm beginning to think it's impossible," Caru said.

Jess came into the kitchen with two pizza boxes.

"What's impossible?" she asked, catching the tail end of their conversation. She set the boxes down and Caru met Charlie's gaze. She shook her head.

"Getting her room tidy," Charlie said. "She's just got too much stuff."

Caru raised an eyebrow at Charlie and he shrugged slightly. To be fair, she couldn't have come up with anything else to say.

"Well duh," Jess said, losing interest quickly. "Dive in everyone," she said, waving at the boxes with the slice of pizza already in her hand.

Caru took her box and moved to the sofa, grabbing some kitchen towel for her greasy fingers on the way. She opened the box and picked up a slice, but she really wasn't very hungry anymore. All she could think about was whether she would ever see Peter again.

CHAPTER TWENTY FOUR

"CHARLIE and I have an announcement to make."

Caru looked up from her dinner at Jess, who was addressing the whole table of their friends who had gathered for an impromptu meal.

Jess looked at Charlie who was grinning at her. "We're getting married."

Caru's eyes bugged out and she was glad she didn't have a mouthful of food to choke on. "Oh my goodness," she said, getting up to hug her housemate. "That's amazing!"

She then hugged Charlie, and everyone got up to hug the couple. Caru felt a little shocked. It was so fast. They had only been seeing each other for less than two months. But she had to admit, she'd never seen two people so happy together. And with Charlie's newly released single set to become Christmas number one, things were definitely looking rosy for them.

She was so happy for them, but she couldn't help feeling a little hollow.

Despite insisting that she just had to get used to life without Peter, after several weeks of being back in her old life, she was still grieving the loss of him. She had thrown herself into her work, and had cleared out her room, and begun saving to open her own shop. In the meantime, she had started her online shop, and she'd already had a few sales in the run up to Christmas. There was still two weeks to go, so she hoped to have a few more last minute sales.

She'd also received an early Christmas gift the week before when her copy of *Pressing Matters* magazine had arrived with her article published in it. It had taken her by surprise, seeing the words she had written before the shift printed alongside images of her work and a photo of herself. She had stared at her own face, seeing a completely different person to the one she had become.

Her words now had an entirely different meaning to her as she realised just how much she had taken for granted in her old life and also in her alternate life. In this reality, she swore she would enjoy every moment, and never miss a chance to tell the people she loved how much they meant to her.

Without thinking it through, she stood up and tapped her knife against her glass. The chatter around the table stopped and everyone looked at her.

"I just wanted to say how very excited I am for Jess and Charlie, and how much I love them both. It's a rare thing to find the person who fits you, who makes your heart feel lighter, who brings you joy and laughter. And I really couldn't be happier that you two found one another, and are making this commitment to each other."

Jess and Charlie smiled at each other, and Jess leaned towards him and rested her head on his shoulder.

"We may never know the impact that we have on each other's lives, or on the lives of the people we meet briefly out in the world, and perhaps that is a good thing. But I know for certain that acts of kindness never go to waste, and are always worth it."

Charlie was frowning at her slightly, because he knew that her own acts of kindness hadn't necessarily positively impacted her.

"So I would like to propose a toast. To love, kindness, rare connections and seizing the moment. And of course, to the beautiful couple I am proud to call my friends." Caru raised her glass and everyone followed suit, clinking them against each other's glasses. She sat down and met Jess's gaze.

"Thank you," Jess mouthed, wiping her eyes with her napkin.

Caru smiled back.

Caru was busy printing another new line of greeting cards in her room when she heard the front door open.

"Honey! We're home!"

She smiled and wiped her inky hands with a rag before going out to the kitchen.

Jess was putting the kettle on, and she turned to grin at Caru. "We got some great bargains. Charlie has pretty much a whole new wardrobe too."

Caru looked over at Charlie who was sitting at the counter looking exhausted. "She is a ninja shopper, I've never spent so much on clothes for myself before. We were supposed to be Christmas shopping, but I don't think we bought a single gift for anyone."

Jess kissed him and he smiled. "There's still time for that! Christmas is a whole week away. And with your song at number one, we can't have you looking scruffy if the paparazzi come snapping."

Charlie laughed. "I would be amazed if they found me here. And we still don't know for sure if it's going to be number one, there's some strong competition."

"Well, you're always number one to me!" Jess said, kissing him on the forehead.

"Did you find a ring?" Caru asked, pouring the hot water onto her tea bag.

"Not yet," Jess said. "Apparently I'm very picky, but I think it's more that I have super expensive taste."

Charlie nodded. "She really does. I need a Christmas number one to afford her."

Jess grinned at Caru and she smiled back. "Let's hope for the number one slot then," Caru said, chuckling.

There was a beep and Jess pulled out her phone and looked at it. Her face twisted into a frown. "Ugh, I'm so glad that I'm not on Pyre anymore. There are some sick weirdos out there."

"What is it?" Caru said, looking for something to eat in her cupboard.

"Some guy hooked up with a woman on Pyre, moved into her house, then tried to beat her."

Caru's hand that was reaching for a pack of crackers went still. Surely it couldn't be?

"But he had no idea that she was a former black belt in taekwondo. She beat his ass, and then reported him to the police. He's been charged with domestic violence charges."

Caru's heart beat quickened. "Does it say what his name is?"

"Um," Jess scanned back through the article. "Henry Mathews."

Caru dropped the crackers she had picked up. They landed on the counter with a soft thud, no doubt shattering the whole packet into a million pieces. She turned around and held her hand out. "Can I see?"

Jess shrugged and handed over her phone, and began rummaging through her shopping bags.

Caru read the article, and couldn't believe it when she saw Henry's face, complete with black eye. She was so thankful that he hadn't managed to hurt the woman. She hoped that now he was known to the police he wouldn't be able to kill anyone.

She put the phone down on the counter.

"You okay, Caru? You look like you've seen a ghost." Charlie said, sounding concerned.

She breathed in deeply and nodded.

"I'm okay, it just scares me, this kind of thing." She hugged Jess, who was a little surprised. "I'm very glad that you aren't on Pyre now too. And that you guys are together. I really do think you make an amazing couple." Before she could get too emotional, she picked up her tea, muttered that she needed to get back to her printing, and left the kitchen, leaving Charlie and Jess looking at each other with puzzled looks.

Caru was settling down on the sofa with a blanket and a bucket of popcorn when Jess and Charlie came into the kitchen.

"Are you sure you're okay here on your own?" Jess asked again.

"I'm positive. Go to the party, you guys need to have fun." She waved the remote at the TV. "I have a Fringe marathon ahead of me."

"Are you sure you're okay?" Charlie asked. He had a concerned look on his face again.

"I'm fine, just a bit worn out from working too much over the last few weeks. I just need a bit of rest, I think."

Jess came over and kissed her on the head. "Be good, call us if you need us," she said. For once, it felt like Jess was the mother and she was child. It felt nice to be cared for.

"Have fun," Caru called out.

Jess and Charlie left when the buzzer sounded to tell them their taxi had arrived. They had been invited to a fancy Christmas party with some other musicians, so they wouldn't be back until the early hours.

Caru was well into season three of Fringe where the episodes started switching between universes, when her phone beeped. She picked it up and scanned the message then sighed. Kevin really didn't know the meaning of taking the night off. He wanted to have a meeting with her in the morning before the gallery opened about the line-up for the Spring Exhibition. Which they had already finalised the week before. She tapped a reply back, saying that she could be there for nine (she was going to need a strong coffee first) and then she put her phone on silent, so she could watch Peter fall in love with Olivia from the other universe.

CHAPTER TWENTY FIVE

WHEN Caru arrived at the gallery at quarter past nine the next morning, she found Kevin in a whirl of activity, rearranging paintings on the wall.

"Sorry I'm late," she said, sipping her coffee. "Bus was late." She watched him for a few moments. "Everything okay?"

"Yes, sorry, I just wanted to try a different arrangement, I feel like these pieces have been hidden away at the back here, and they need to be more prominent. There's still a week of possible sales before Christmas."

Caru headed behind the counter and took off her coat, scarf and hat. "Okay, but you know we will be changing the whole display right after New Year's though?"

"Yeah, of course, I just thought it might help."

"Or you just couldn't sit still for five minutes and chill," Caru teased. "Promise me you will try to relax just a little bit over Christmas? I know I'm busy most of the time but you make even me look lazy."

Kevin chuckled. "Okay, I promise I will try."

Caru shook her head and sipped more coffee. "So what was the emergency? We have the line up for spring, has someone dropped out?"

Kevin shook his head as he adjusted a framed print to get it hanging straight. "No, I've just discovered a new one, and we need to squeeze him in."

"Squeeze him in? We already have too many pieces."

"I know, but his work, it's just, well, there's no other word for it. It's magical."

Caru raised an eyebrow. Kevin wasn't known for his interest in anything otherworldly.

"Magical? In what way? Who is it?"

"It's this unknown artist who up until three months ago, painted fairly boring landscapes, but he is exhibiting his new pieces which are just something else entirely. According to him, he painted them all within three days, after having an odd dream." Kevin shrugged. "You know how artists are. Anyway, I *need* to have the pieces in the Spring Exhibition."

Kevin looked at Caru, his eyes pleading.

She sighed. "Okay, fine, I will work out a new plan for the layout. Do you know which pieces we're having? If you give me the information I'll get the labels done. Because I am not doing any work over Christmas. I am relaxing for once. I'm seeing Laura and the kids, and just chilling out."

Kevin dug in his bag and handed her a piece of paper then stole a sip of her coffee. "Ugh, no sugar," he muttered, setting it back down.

Caru smoothed out the crumpled paper and flicked the

computer on. She opened up the label printing software and began typing in the details. When she reached the artist's name, her heart thumped a little harder. P Phillips. Surely it couldn't be? She thought of Peter's murals in the nursery, and his incessant doodling. She typed in the rest of the details, and printed the label. Then she input the next title. When she reached the third label, she frowned.

"Do you have any photos of the paintings?" she asked.

Kevin shook his head, busy lining up another painting. "No I didn't bother taking any. Why?"

"No reason, would just be interested to see them. Are they all of the same person? There seems to be a theme."

"Yeah, same person I think." He looked over at Caru. "The exhibition is still on until tomorrow, you could go and check them out if you want. I chatted to Peter for a while, lovely guy, seems really down to earth."

"Peter?" Caru echoed, her heart thumping a little faster.

"Yeah, he uses just his initial for his artwork. I would say look online, but there's not much on there, just a basic website with a few of his landscapes on there."

Caru opened up a browser on the computer and typed in his name and 'artist'. His website popped up and she saw that Kevin was right, there was scant information. But when she read his bio, her eyes widened. "He did a degree in archaeology," she said.

"Oh, yeah he mentioned that. Said that he was all set to go down that path when a close friend of his died suddenly, and he realised that he wanted to follow his dreams instead. So he became an artist."

Caru tried to breathe deeply and slowly, and to not get her hopes up again, because she wasn't sure she could cope with the disappointment.

But what if it was him?

She clicked on the Events tab, and took note of where the exhibition was taking place. Tomorrow was indeed the last day, and luckily, it was her day off. She had planned to go Christmas shopping, but she knew that she couldn't miss the opportunity to go and see the exhibition. What if it really was him?

At ten o'clock, she put the sign out, opened the door and did her best to convince Kevin to stop rearranging the paintings. She tried to do some sketches for new card designs, but all she could think about was what might happen the next day.

"You're in a rush," Jess commented as Caru dashed around the kitchen, eating toast and doing up the buttons on her top.

Caru swallowed the mouthful of bread and jam and nodded. "Art exhibition, just, um, really excited to see it."

Jess raised an eyebrow. "Must be some amazing art, or maybe a hot artist?" she said hopefully.

Caru blushed but managed to hide her face from her housemate as she ate the rest of her toast and dashed back out of the kitchen. "See you later!" she called out. She went into her room to grab her gloves and scarf. Even after a couple of weeks, it was still a bit of a shock to find her room in a neat state. It wasn't as immaculate as her room from her other life, but it was neat and tidy, with no clothes on the floor, or half-finished projects spilling out of every drawer and cupboard. And her bed was always neatly made, with a quilt her mum had made her as a child on the top of the bedspread.

She grabbed her hat and gloves and then turned off the light and headed out the door, grabbing her heavy winter coat on the way. It had been a mild December up until a few days before, and now it was feeling quite bitter. She had quite a walk from where the bus would drop her off to where the exhibition was, so she wanted to be warm.

Luckily, the bus was right on time, which was something of a miracle, and she was glad not to have to wait too long at the bus stop. She stared out of the window, feeling jittery and impatient. She had barely slept the night before, feeling a mixture of excitement, nerves, anxiety and hope. Hope that it was really him. Hope that it wasn't. Because if it was him, and there was no spark, she worried that it would be even more crushing than if it wasn't him at all.

Her mind a whir, she glanced out of the window and noticed that they were close by, so she got up and went to the front of the bus. "Next stop please," she said to the driver.

He inclined his head.

She held on tight to the pole as they went round a sharp corner, and then stumbled forward a few steps when the bus came to an abrupt halt.

"Thanks," she said to the driver.

"Hope you find what you're looking for," the driver replied.

Caru turned around as the doors closed, and she could have sworn the bus driver winked at her.

She consulted the map on her phone, and found that she was actually a lot closer to the venue than she thought she would be. In fact, she was barely a five minute walk from it. She glanced around. There was no bus stop sign.

"How does he know?" she muttered to herself as she set off in the right direction.

A few minutes later, she came to the old renovated church that was now an art gallery and studio space. She paused for a moment, and tried to convince herself that it didn't matter if it wasn't him. That she was just going because it was a new artist that they were representing and that it was just a work thing.

But she couldn't bullshit herself. Her heart was pounding, her palms were sweaty and her mouth was completely dry.

Before she could be spotted standing outside muttering to herself, Caru went up to the heavy front door and pushed it open. She was greeted with a welcoming blast of dry, warm air. She slipped in around the door and pushed it closed again, then paused for a moment in the hallway to remove her gloves and hat, and tuck them into her bag. She ran a hand through her hair, checked her minimal makeup in her tiny compact mirror, then took a deep breath and headed to the door leading to the main gallery space.

When she stepped inside, she was greeted by a young woman who was holding out a glass of mulled wine to her, which Caru accepted gratefully along with a leaflet for the exhibition. She wrapped her cold fingers around the warm glass, and smiled her thanks, tucking the leaflet into her bag. Then she turned to look at the first painting on the wall, and was thankful that she had a good grip on the red liquid, otherwise it would have been tricky to clean out of the worn wooden floorboards.

The first painting was of a woman in a garden, her long brown hair floating on the breeze, brightly coloured flowers behind her. Caru moved closer, her breathing slightly ragged. The title on the label said – *The Girl in the Garden.* She studied the image for a while, the impressionistic style hiding the identity of the woman, yet speaking volumes about her at the same time. Kevin was right. These paintings were magical.

She moved onto the next piece. *The Girl in the Restaurant.* In this one, she could see more of the woman's face. Her expression. Her smile. She could also see the shapes of fake cacti in the background, and the colourful dishes of salsa and guacamole.

Heart pounding so loudly, Caru wondered if the other people in the room could hear it, she moved onto the next piece.

The Girl in the Castle.

The Girl in the Nursery.

The Girl in the Art Gallery.

While looking at the final piece, tears began to pool in her eyes, and she heard a camera shutter clicking behind her. She turned around to find a guy snapping her photo.

"Oh, hey, sorry, I couldn't resist. You just looked exactly like the photo! Kind of like a dream within a dream sort of thing. Anyway, I'm doing a piece on the exhibition for the local paper, would you mind if I used your photo?"

Caru blinked away her tears and shook her head. "No, it's fine."

The guy grinned. "Excellent, thanks." He glanced around and looked back at her. "You know, you really do look a heck of a lot like the girl in these paintings."

Caru looked around the room. "Yeah, I guess I do."

"Oh, there's the artist." The photographer was looking at someone in the doorway. "Hey, Peter, I've found your girl!"

Caru closed her eyes. This was it. This was the moment. Considering that the room was filled with memories of the other life, she couldn't see how it couldn't be her Peter. But there was always some small chance that the Universe was playing a cruel trick on her.

She turned slowly and opened her eyes to look at the artist.

When she met his gaze, he stopped in his tracks.

The photographer, distracted by another person arriving, wandered off, and carried on snapping photos of the exhibition.

"Hi, Peter," Caru said, trying to keep her voice from wavering.

"Hi," Peter said, moving closer. He studied her face, then looked up at the painting nearest them. "You do look like her," he said. "Uncannily so."

Caru smiled. "My name is Caru," she said. "I work at Flamingo Fine Art."

"Oh, sure, yeah I met Kevin the day before yesterday. Great guy, said he wanted to show my work in the Spring Exhibition."

"Yes, he told me your work was magical, so I just had to see them for myself."

"Well it's nice to meet you, Caru," Peter said, holding out his hand.

Caru shook his hand, her palm tingling at their touch. Peter frowned, and held onto her hand for a few moments longer.

Finally, he released her hand and smiled at her. "What

do you think of the exhibition?"

Caru tried not to show her disappointment. She was so sure that he would have been able to recognise her touch. "It's great, I really like it. What inspired it?" She figured that maybe getting him to remember his dream would help.

Peter grinned and shook his head. "You'll think I'm crazy. I'm pretty sure Kevin thought I was nuts."

"Try me," Caru said softly.

"It was about three months ago, I woke up from the most intense and vivid dream where I was in a relationship," he waved at the painting in front of them. "With her." He shook his head. "I could simultaneously feel how much I loved her, while being overwhelmed with the grief of losing her. And in a bid to remember, I started painting. And I didn't stop for three days."

Caru's eyes were beginning to fill with tears again, but she blinked them away rapidly, trying not to let them fall.

Peter sighed. "It was a bit crazy, but I had this feeling that if I created these paintings, and exhibited them, that somehow, she would come back to me."

Caru bit her lip, and tried to hold in the giggle that was now bubbling up inside. 'Peter!' she thought impatiently. 'It's me!'

"It's not crazy at all," she said. "Tell me about the paintings, about what you remember."

"Really? You have time?"

"I have nowhere else I need to be," Caru replied honestly.

"Okay, well we have to begin with this one, *The Girl in Peru*. Because it was the first thing I painted, and it was the vaguest memory of them all because I feel like it was just a memory of a memory. Which probably makes no sense."

Caru stared at the girl in brightly coloured clothes, camera around her neck, in Machu Picchu. "You don't remember this moment clearly?"

"No. But it feels like the beginning somehow."

"Maybe that's where you met her," Caru suggested, smiling to herself.

Peter frowned and squinted at the painting, as if he were trying to see the image in more detail. "Yeah, that feels right. The first time I met her…"

"Perhaps you helped her," Caru said, wondering how far she would have to nudge before he finally recognised her.

Peter didn't respond. He turned from the painting to Caru, then back again. "I think you're right again. I think there was a situation, and I… saved her."

Caru smiled. "Yes, you did."

Peter looked at her, confusion evident on his face. "Caru. That's the Welsh word for love." He frowned at the painting. "That's what she said to me. In Peru. In my dream."

Caru's smile became wider and her eyes sparkled with tears as Peter studied her face.

"Caru," he whispered. "It wasn't a dream, was it?" His voice was filled with shock and wonder.

"No," she replied. "It was very real."

"But, but," Peter looked around the room again that was filled with memories of their life together. "How?"

Caru laughed and pulled a tissue out of her bag to wipe her eyes. "That really is the question. And I have no idea what the answer is. But we did have a life together in another world to this one. And I never meant to leave you there. I hope you know that."

Peter frowned. "Leave me there… so our life together ended when you returned to this reality?" He looked like he couldn't quite believe he was saying the words.

Caru nodded. "Yes, I think so. I didn't mean to leave, but I think I had learnt all I needed to. I've been searching for you since that moment, but your resistance to social media made it quite impossible."

Peter groaned. "I'm sorry, I know I should move with the times. I would have searched for you, but I had nothing concrete to search for. Just these memories."

"You captured them perfectly," Caru said, looking around the room.

"I wish I hadn't sold so many pieces now though."

"Don't worry," Caru moved closer to him, and breathed in his scent. "We can make new memories."

Peter brought her hand up to his chest. He looked shocked but happy. "I think I'd like that very much," he said. "Starting with now?"

Caru smiled up at him, then reached up to meet him halfway as he leaned down to kiss her.

EPLIOGUE

"THIS is the last piece from *The Girl* Exhibition by P. Phillips," Caru explained to the customer who was staring at *The Girl in Peru*. She was sad that it might sell, she had enjoyed looking at it over the last few months.

The customer nodded and continued to browse, and Caru wandered back to the desk. The Spring Exhibition was well underway, and the pieces were selling well. Peter's work had been popular, and he was now working on a new series, based on the new memories they were now creating.

Caru rested her hand on her stomach. No one knew yet, except the two of them, that those memories would soon involve a baby.

Her experiences in the other life had prepared her, and this time she started avoiding onions as soon as she found out. But the sickness hadn't been too bad this time.

"I'll take it."

Caru looked up at the customer and smiled. "Excellent, I'll get it wrapped up for you, card or cash?"

After taking the payment and wrapping up the piece, Caru watched the customer go, taking the last piece of her other life with them. It was weird, but she felt some closure. Like she could move on knowing that the other life was over now.

Jess and Charlie were alive. Laura had Rob and the children. She had found Peter and was making a new life for herself.

Things were finally all falling into place.

At four o'clock, she brought the sign in, switched off all the lights, and locked up for the day. She and Peter were going out for a meal to celebrate the success of his exhibition with Jess and Charlie who were also celebrating. Charlie's latest song had hit number one. *Faith in a Teacup* had been the Christmas number one, and had stayed in the charts for two months afterwards. And his new single, *The Girl Who Loved Too Much*, was set to break that record.

Caru smiled as she walked down the high street to the bus stop, the new song playing in her head. Charlie had been inspired by Caru and Peter's reunion. She whispered the lyrics out loud to herself.

"A dream within a dream,
Another world, same souls,
Destined to collide together,
Two parts of a whole."

Caru was only waiting at the bus stop for a few minutes before it arrived, and she got on board still humming to herself. It had been a blissful three months, being with Peter again. He had pretty much moved in with Caru, and was using the spare room as his art studio. With Charlie living in Jess's room, the small flat was bursting at the seams. But it wouldn't be for too much longer. Jess and Charlie were in the process of buying their first home together. And she and Peter had begun saving up as well. But in the meantime, they would stay at the flat. Her plans to open her own shop were on hold for now, but she had been printing more ranges of cards and prints, and had branched out. She was now supplying fifteen gift shops around the country with her work.

The bus jolted as it hit a pothole, shaking Caru out of her daydream. She looked around and realised her stop was next. She rang the bell and got up, picking up her bag and moving to the front of the bus as it rolled to a stop.

Before she could thank the driver, he spoke.

"You were given a gift," he said. "I'm glad you used it well."

Caru turned to look at him and he winked at her.

"Thank you," she said, wondering again whether it had been him all along.

"Just be sure to enjoy it," he replied with a smile.

She nodded, and stepped off the bus. As she walked up the lane to her home, she chuckled to herself.

It seemed this had all been the work of a magical bus driver after all.

She just hoped she would stay in this reality from now on. It was a beautiful one. And it would only get better.

She was sure of it.

ABOUT THE AUTHOR

Michelle lives in the UK, when she's not flitting in and out of other realms. She is an avid crafter, and enjoys letterpress printing, knitting, sewing, crochet, photography and many other creative pursuits. She has so far written fifteen novels for adults, one for children, a poetry collection and a self-help book.

Please feel free to write a review of this book. Michelle loves to get direct feedback, so if you would like to contact her, please e-mail **theamethystangel@hotmail.co.uk** or keep up to date by following her blog – **TwinFlameBlog.com.** You can also follow her on Twitter **@themiraclemuse** or on Instagram **@michellegordonauthor**

To sign up to her mailing list, visit:

MICHELLEGORDON.CO.UK

LINKS

PRESSING MATTERS MAGAZINE

pressingmattersmag.com
Instagram - @pressingmattersmag

LYME BAY PRESS

lymebaypress.co.uk
Instagram - @lymebaypress

CREATES GALLERY

createsgallery.com
Instagram - @createsgallery

BERRINGTON PRESS

berrington-press.co.uk
Instagram - @berrington_press

QUARTO 17

quarto17.etsy.com
Instagram - @francesca_kay

MARIE KONDO

konmari.com
Instagram - @mariekondo

MAGIC LETTERPRESS

Instagram - @magic_letterpress

BOOKS BY MICHELLE GORDON

WHERE'S MY F**KING UNICORN?

Are your bookshelves filled with self-help books, and yet your life feels empty? Do you keep following paths to enlightenment that lead to the same dead ends? You've read the books, attended the seminars and taken heed of every bit of advice going... but you're still waiting for your f**king unicorn to come along! Where's My F**king Unicorn? is a guide to life, creativity and happiness that offers a very different way forward. Author, Michelle Gordon, explains why, in spite of all your best efforts, your life still doesn't live up to your vision of what it should be, and tells you exactly what you can do about it. In refreshingly down-to-earth language, she shows you how to harness all the self-knowledge you have gained from all those self-help books you've read, and actually start putting it to practical use.

EARTH ANGEL SERIES

THE EARTH ANGEL TRAINING ACADEMY

(book 1)

There are humans on Earth, who are not, in fact, human.

They are **Earth Angels**.

Earth Angels are beings who have come from other realms, dimensions and planets, and are choosing to be born on Earth in human form for just **one** reason.

To **Awaken the world**.

Before they can carry out their perilous mission, they must first learn how to be human.

The best place they can do that, is at

The Earth Angel Training Academy

THE EARTH ANGEL AWAKENING

(book 2)

After learning how to be human at the Earth Angel Training Academy, the Angels, Faeries, Merpeople and Starpeople are born into human bodies on Earth.

Their Mission? **Awaken the world**.

But even though they **chose** to go to Earth, and they chose to be human, it doesn't mean that it will be **easy** for them to Awaken themselves.

Only if they **reconnect** to their **origins**, and to other Earth Angels, will they will be able to **remember** who they really are.

Only then, will they experience

The Earth Angel Awakening

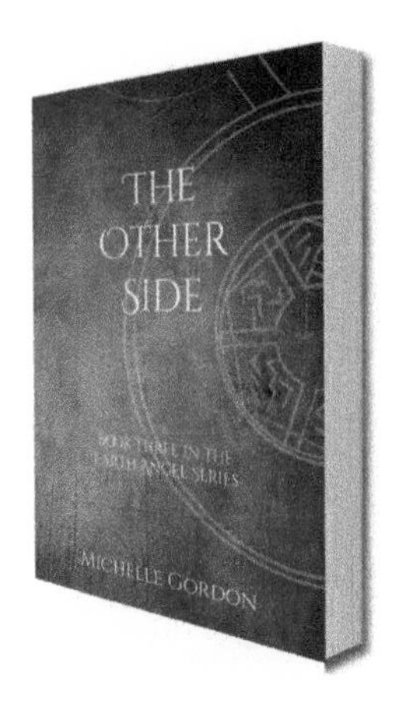

THE OTHER SIDE

(book 3)

There is an Angel who holds the world in her hands.
She is the **Angel of Destiny**.
Her actions will start the **ripples** that will **save humans** from their certain demise.
In order for her to initiate the necessary changes, she must travel to other **galaxies**, and call upon the most **enlightened** and **evolved** beings of the Universe.
To save **humankind**.
When they agree, she wishes to prepare them for Earth life, and so invites them to attend the Earth Angel Training Academy, on

The Other Side

THE TWIN FLAME REUNION

(book 4)

The Earth Angels' missions are clear: **Awaken** the world, and move humanity into the **Golden Age**.

But there is another reason many of the Earth Angels choose to come to Earth.

To **reunite** with their **Twin Flames**.

The Twin Flame connection is deep, everlasting and intense, and happens only at the **end of an age**. Many Flames have not been together for millennia, some have never met.

Once on Earth, every Earth Angel longs to meet their Flame. The one who will make them **feel at home**, who will make living on this planet bearable.

But no one knows if they will actually get to experience

The Twin Flame Reunion

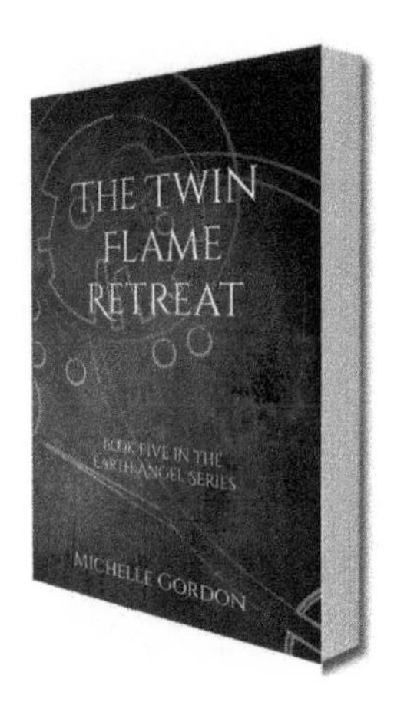

THE TWIN FLAME RETREAT

(book 5)

The question in the minds of many Earth Angels
on Earth right now is:
Where is my **Twin Flame?**
Though many Earth Angels are now meeting their Flames,
the circumstances around their reunion can have
life-altering consequences.
If meeting your Flame meant your life would never be the
same again, would you still want to find them?
When in need of **support** and answers,
Earth Angels attend
The Twin Flame Retreat

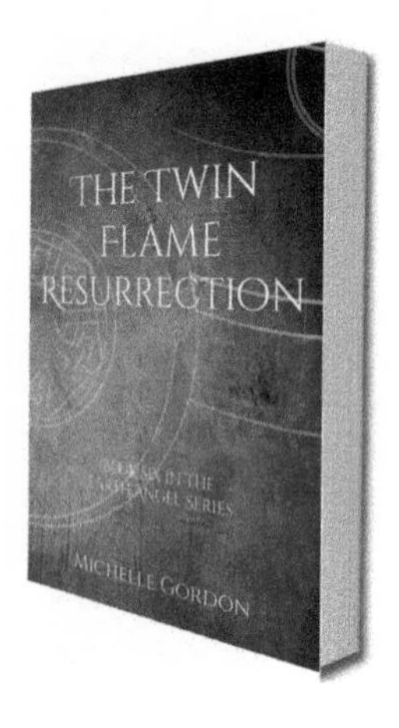

THE TWIN FLAME RESURRECTION

(book 6)

Twin Flames are **destined** to meet. And when they are meant to be together, nothing can keep them apart.

Not even **death**.

When Earth Angels go home to the Fifth Dimension too soon, they have the **choice** to come back.

To be with their **Twin Flame**.

The connection can be so overwhelming, that some Earth Angels try to resist it, try to push it away.

But it is **undeniable**.

When things don't go according to plan, the universe steps in, and the Earth Angels experience

The Twin Flame Ressurrection

THE TWIN FLAME REALITY

(book 7)

Being an Earth Angel on Earth can be difficult, especially when it doesn't feel like home, and when there's a deep longing for a realm or dimension where you feel you **belong**.

Finding a Twin Flame, is like **coming home**.

Losing one, can be **devastating**.

Adrift, lonely, isolated... an Earth Angel would be forgiven for preferring to go home, than to stay here **without their Flame**.

But if they can find the **strength** to stay, to follow their mission to **Awaken** the world, and fulfil their original purpose, they will find they can be **happy** here.

Even despite the sadness of

The Twin Flame Reality

THE TWIN FLAME REBELLION

(book 8)

The Angels on the Other Side have a **duty** to **help** their human charges, but **only** when they are **asked** for help. They are not allowed to meddle with **Free Will**.

But a number of Angels are asked to break their **Golden Rule**, and start influencing the human lives of the Earth Angels.

Once the Angels start nudging, they find they can't stop, and when the Earth Angels find out they are being manipulated from the Other Side, they aren't happy.

Determined to **choose** their own **fate**, the Earth Angels embark on

The Twin Flame Rebellion

THE TWIN FLAME REIGNITION

(book 9)

The **destiny** of many **Twin Flames** is changing.
Those destined to remain apart on Earth are hearing the call to come **together.**
As things begin to shift and change, it suddenly it seems **possible** for them to **reunite,** and have the lives they always **dreamed** of.
But when **visions** and **dreams** of **Atlantis** begin to plague the Earth Angels, and they try to work out their meaning, what they **discover** may jeopardise
The Twin Flame Reignition

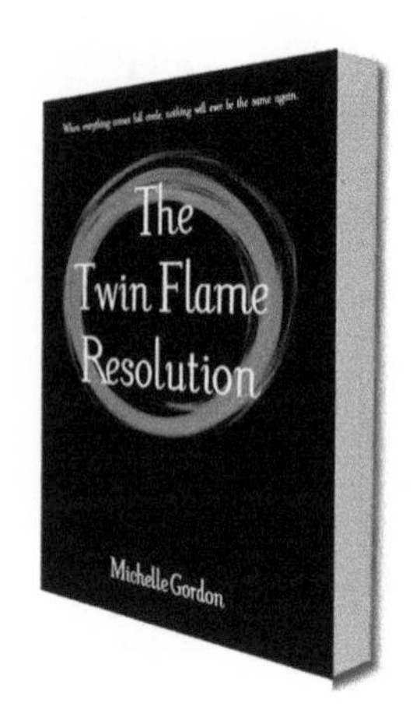

THE TWIN FLAME RESOLUTION

(book 10)

When a Seer has a **vision** of the **Golden Age**, she takes drastic action in order to make it happen.
The consequences of her actions are so **epic** that the lives of every **Earth Angel** and every **human** on Earth will be altered **forever.**
As well as the unions of all the
Twin Flames.
She enlists the help of two **Angels** to assist her in
The Twin Flame Resolution

VISIONARY COLLECTION

Heaven dot com

When Christina goes into hospital for the final time, and knows that she is about to lose her battle with cancer, she asks her boyfriend, James, to help her deliver messages to her family and friends after she has gone.

She also asks him to do something for her, but she dies before he can make it happen, and he finds it difficult to forgive himself.

After her death, her messages are received by her loved ones, and the impact her words have will change their lives forever.

The Doorway to PAM

Natalie is an ordinary girl who has lost her way. There is nothing particularly special about her or her life. She has no exceptional abilities. She hasn't achieved anything miraculous. Her life has very little meaning to it.

Evelyn is the caretaker at Pam's. The alternate dimension where souls at their lowest point find the answers they need to turn their lives around. The dimension dreamers visit, to help people while they sleep.

One ordinary girl, one extraordinary woman.
One fated meeting that will change lives.

The Elphite

Ellie's life is just one long, bad case of déjà vu. She has lived her life before - a hundred times before - and she remembers each and every lifetime.
Each time, she has changed things, but has never managed to change the ending.
This time, in this life, she hopes that it will be different.
So she makes the biggest change of all - she tries to avoid meeting him.
Her soulmate. The love of her life.
Because maybe if they don't meet, she can finally change her destiny.
But fate has other ideas...

I'm Here

When Marielle finds out that a guy she had a crush on in school has passed away, the strange occurrences of the previous week begin to make sense. She suspects that he is trying to give her a message from the other side, and so opens up to communicate with him, She has no idea that by doing so, she will be forming a bond so strong, that life as she knows it will forever be changed.

Nathan assumed that when he died, he would move on, and continue his spiritual journey. But instead he finds himself drawn to a girl that he once knew. The more he watches her, and gets to know her, he realises that he was drawn to her for a reason, and that once he knows what that is, he will be able to change his destiny.

The Visionary Collection is published by *The Amethyst Angel* and is available online in eBook and print.

Duelling Poets

For 30 days in 2012, Michelle Gordon and Victor Keegan wrote a poem a day, taking turns to choose the titles.

Michelle is an author, who was in her late 20s at the time, and Victor, a retired journalist in his 70s. Their differing experiences and perspectives created contrasting poems, despite being written about the same topic.

In Duelling Poets, we invite you to read the poems and choose your favourites, then at the end, you can see which poet wins the duel for you.

Little Something is published by *Labradorite Press* and is available online in eBook and print.

Not From This Planet is an Independent Publisher on a mission to collaborate with authors to create the best possible books that delight and inspire and entertain – and also pay a fair royalty to the author. They treat every book as if it were their own and they have big have plans to take the publishing world by storm.

Follow Not From This Planet on
Instagram - @notfromthisplanetbooks
Facebook - @notfromthisplanetbooks
Twitter - @ NFTPbooks

NotFromThisPlanet.co.uk

Lightning Source UK Ltd.
Milton Keynes UK
UKHW012012221120
373896UK00002B/66